Books by Mavis Jukes

Blackberries in the Dark
Getting Even
Lights Around the Palm
Like Jake and Me
No One Is Going to Nashville
Wild Iris Bloom

Wild Iris Bloom

by Mavis Jukes

Alfred A. Knopf
New York

THIS IS A BORZOI BOOK PUBLISHED BY ALFRED A. KNOPF, INC.

Library of Congress Cataloging-in-Publication Data
Jukes, Mavis. Wild Iris Bloom / Mavis Jukes. p. cm.
    Summary: Independent-minded and angry at being left at home while
her parents travel on business, twelve-year-old Iris gives her
babysitter the slip; but a disturbing incident makes her realize
that she does need her family and friends.
ISBN 0-679-81891-X (trade) — ISBN 0-679-91891-4 (lib. bdg.)
[1. Babysitters—Fiction.   2.Child molesting—Fiction.]
I. Title. PZ7.J9294Wi 1992 [Fic]—dc20 90-24315

10 9 8 7 6 5 4 3 2 1

Manufactured in the United States of America

To the Kneuppels:
Caroline, Nick, Elizabeth,
and John—with love
—M. J.

Wild Iris Bloom

ONE

Mrs. Fuller squirted something from a plastic container onto the woodwork around Iris's bedroom door. She rubbed the woodwork with a cloth. "Elbow grease!" she said, and grunted.

Iris pulled a *Mad* magazine out from under the leg of her chair and began leafing through it.

"On TV they never say anything about elbow grease! They never show how hard you have to scrub off the dirt—they just show a sponge gliding over it . . . ."

Iris peered at Mrs. Fuller above the top of the magazine.

". . . softly held by a beautiful hand with red fingernail polish and a twinkly ring—"

The phone rang. Mrs. Fuller hurried into the hall and picked it up.

"Eee-yellow," Iris heard her say. "Bloom residence. Edna Fuller speaking. . . ."

Iris tossed the magazine over her shoulder and stood up.

"One moment, please. . . . Phone for you!" bellowed Mrs. Fuller.

"I'm right here," said Iris.

"It's Maggie Hunter."

Iris took the receiver. Mrs. Fuller stood there, staring at her.

"It's me," said Maggie. "Mom says I can invite you to come with us to the mall this afternoon."

Iris covered the mouthpiece. "I'm going with Maggie to the mall. Okay?"

"Not alone you're not!"

"With her mother," said Iris.

"What time?" said Mrs. Fuller. "I'm making pigs in blankets for dinner!"

"Mrs. Fuller wants to know what time," said Iris to Maggie.

"Now," said Maggie. "And Iris?"

"What?"

Maggie lowered her voice. "You know what I told you about what's happening in March . . ."

"About your dad and Samantha getting married?" said Iris.

She looked at Mrs. Fuller. "We're going in a few minutes," she said. "Okay?"

"Okay," said Mrs. Fuller.

Iris waited for Mrs. Fuller to leave, but she just stood there, listening.

"Well, I just was going to say," said Maggie, "let's not talk about it in front of my mom. I mean, it's not like it's a big secret or anything—but I don't know." She paused. "It kind of . . . bums her out."

"Well, I won't say anything," said Iris. She glanced at Mrs. Fuller. "I wouldn't say anything about something like that, anyway."

"I know," said Maggie. "But I just wanted to—oh, I don't know! Anyway . . ." Maggie lowered her voice. "You should see the dress I'm wearing. It's a drop-waist. Samantha picked it out. Samantha said I'm a little 'underdeveloped' for the cut. It's a 'junior bridesmaid—' "

"A *little* underdeveloped?" said Iris.

"—but she can alter it," said Maggie.

"Yes, I'm sure she can cut a few . . . yards of material out of the top," said Iris. "What color is it?"

"Blue with, like, ruffles. But the ruffles come down too low on top."

Iris smiled a little. "Well, you're not president of The Flat People's Club for nothing, you know."

"Anyway, we'll see you in a few minutes," said Maggie.

"Okay," said Iris. She hung up the phone and ran into her bedroom. Thank heavens Maggie had mentioned developing! She kicked some stuff away from her closet door and pulled it open.

Where was her camera? She needed to take a picture of her room in its latest stage of disorder. She was making a flip book for her art class and had already shot almost two rolls of film. The first picture was of her room on the day her parents left for Europe—everything was in place. She had taken a picture every day since. The project was due on Monday.

Cameras and Moore at the mall had one-day developing. She would shoot a couple of final shots and drop off the film at the mall.

If she could find her camera.

And the other roll of film.

"I need money!" Iris cried to Mrs. Fuller. "And my camera! And my film!"

Mrs. Fuller hurried into Iris's room. She looked alarmed.

"Maggie and her mother will be here in five minutes," said Iris. She waded through the sea of papers on the rug.

"Can this be thrown out?" said Mrs. Fuller. She held up a crumpled piece of notebook paper with lipstick kisses on it.

"Nothing can be thrown out until the documentation is complete," said Iris. "Nothing!" She shuffled through the debris on her desktop, knocking a basket of colored pencils and a tube of lipstick onto the floor.

"Isn't that your mother's lipstick?" said Mrs. Fuller.

"There you are!" shouted Iris. She took her camera from around the neck of her huge stuffed gorilla. On his lap, she found the other roll of film.

Iris dumped everything off the seat of a wooden chair and stood on it, waving Mrs. Fuller out of the frame. She took a picture, then hurled her nightgown and her Porsche calendar from the top of her canopy bed onto the rug, and took another one.

"Done," she said. She kissed the camera. "Forty-eight pictures."

She pressed a button; the film buzzed backward. "Can I please have some money? They'll be here any second."

"It's the last of the twenties," said Mrs. Fuller, taking a twenty-dollar bill out of her pocket.

"And I need a ten," said Iris.

"A ten?" Mrs. Fuller groaned. She pulled out another bill. "What do you need thirty dollars for?"

"My sneakers smell like mushrooms," said Iris. She stuffed the money into her pocket and found a purple sweater with the tags still on. Pulling it over her head, she stared through the wool until Mrs. Fuller left the room.

Iris popped her head out of the top. Although she'd grown some over the past couple of months, it wasn't where it mattered, so the sweater was still too big. She pushed the sleeves up, then reached into the neck to yank out the Velcro shoulder pads, which she threw onto the floor. She looked at herself in the mirror and briefly considered putting the shoulder pads into her bra.

She took the sweater off and tossed it on top of her canopy bed. She repegged the bottom of her jeans, folding them over and rolling them up. Then she tucked in her T-shirt, fiddled with her bangs, and spritzed them with hairspray. A horn beeped. "They're here!" she shouted.

Iris grabbed her jacket and raced outside. She hopped into the back seat of the car alongside Maggie's little sister, Dinah.

"Guess what!" cried Dinah. "I quit!"

"When?" said Iris.

Maggie turned around. "She did not."

"Let me see your thumb," said Iris. Dinah held up her thumb; it was wet and wrinkled. *"When* did you quit?" asked Iris.

Dinah said nothing.

"Two minutes ago," said Maggie's mother. She backed out of the driveway. Iris's neighbors, the Blackmans, were sitting on their front porch in rocking chairs.

They waved, and everybody waved back. "You know what?" said Iris. "My friend Fred Brewer is helping his little brother quit sucking his thumb by taping anchovies to his thumbs at night."

"Oh, right," said Maggie.

"He is! He said it's working great—but his brother's sheets stink," said Iris.

"Fred Brewer, huh?" said Maggie's mother, in a sly way. "A new . . . friend?"

"Mom!" said Maggie.

"I'm just asking!" said her mother, innocently. She peered at Iris in the rearview mirror.

"He's my partner in history," said Iris. "We're studying Egypt."

"Uh-huh!" said Maggie's mother. She smiled.

"Mom!" cried Maggie.

"What?" said her mother. She looked over at Maggie. "I'm just saying it's interesting that Iris is studying about Egypt." She looked again at Iris. "Egypt, huh?"

"Yup."

"I wish I was in junior high," said Maggie. "I

hate Franklin Elementary. I hate the sixth grade! I hate Mr. Hoffman!"

"What about your other classes, Iris?" said Maggie's mother.

"In English, we're studying fables. The teacher's making us have a puppet show. It's dumb, and I'm *not* making a puppet."

"Why dumb? It sounds like fun!" said Maggie's mother. "You and Maggie have always liked that kind of thing."

Maggie turned around. "Mom and I are making a stuffed Canadian honker for my grandfather in Vermont."

"Out of underpants and feathers," said Maggie's mother. "And textile paint. We've been having a great time, haven't we, Maggie?"

"Yup, and we made the head and neck out of an old tin bicycle horn—you know, with a rubber squeaker—and covered it with a sock. So when you squeeze it, it honks. We're done, except for the beak," said Maggie.

"You should make a puppet, Iris," said Maggie's mother. "Really! You're an artist! You should take advantage of the creative opportunities at school. You're very clever. You'd dream up something wacky, knowing you—"

"Mom!" said Maggie.

"Well, she would! Iris is *well* known for her . . . inventive mind."

Maggie glanced at Iris. "Well, that's one way of putting it," she said. The car grew quiet. They drove awhile without speaking.

"Made any new friends in the new neighborhood?" said Maggie's mother.

"A family just moved in next door," said Iris. "But I haven't met them. I've only seen them."

"What about old friends? Are a lot of the Franklin kids in your classes?"

"Not really," said Iris. "A few, I guess. In some of my classes I only know about one or two people. I see Hilary. And Stella and Jennifer." She made a face. "Corky Newton's in my English class. And math."

"Lucky you," said Maggie.

"But there's a girl, Nadia, in English, who's talked to me a few times," said Iris. "And a girl named Ceclie, who laughs like a horse. And a cheerleader whose locker is near mine, but she's in the eighth grade. She's like, rully, a Valley Girl. . . ."

"I wish I was in the eighth grade," said Maggie.

"No, you don't," said Iris. "The eighth graders are . . . weird."

"I'd be older than you," said Maggie, in a

dreamy way. "I could boss you around. . . . Anyway, when are your mom and dad coming home? Friday night?"

"Friday morning," said Iris. "And I can hardly wait. Mrs. Fuller has been driving me crazy."

"Well, don't say I said this," said Maggie's mother, "but I can understand how you feel. It *has* been a long trip," she added, sympathetically.

"And Mom's bringing me and Maggie back outfits to wear for our band. Remember, Mag? She said she'd bring us outfits?"

"But when are we going to start practicing?" said Maggie. "We never see each other anymore!"

They parked in the lot near Macy's.

"You said Iris and I get to go around by ourselves," Maggie reminded her mother as they walked into the mall.

"If you keep checking in with me," said Maggie's mother.

"And stay together," said Dinah in a stern voice.

"We will," said Iris.

"And don't talk to strangers," said Dinah.

"We won't," said Iris.

Maggie's mother gave Iris and Maggie instructions about where to meet and headed into the health food store with Dinah.

Iris and Maggie went directly to Cameras and Moore. "Do you have one-day developing?" Iris asked a man with glasses.

He nodded.

"Does it really, like, happen in one day?"

He nodded again.

Iris leaned close to Maggie and whispered in her ear. "Maybe we can drop *you* off here. . . ."

Maggie elbowed her away.

Iris handed the man the film and took the receipt. They headed out of the store and up the tiled stairway. "I need to go to the lingerie store," said Iris.

"Why?" said Maggie. "I thought we were going to Zone Music."

Iris took Maggie by the elbow and hurried her along. "Just for one minute," said Iris.

They walked into Bernadette's. Iris went directly to a rack where some bras were hanging and began pinching the cups.

"Hello," said a woman wearing dark-red lipstick and lots of pancake makeup. "How are we today?"

"Fine," said Maggie.

The woman batted her eyelashes; they were

thickly coated with cobalt-blue mascara. "Can I help you?"

Maggie shyly pointed to Iris.

"My friend needs a padded bra," said Iris, without looking up. "To wear to a wedding."

"No, I don't!" cried Maggie.

Iris held up a large lavender bra on a little plastic hanger and shook it at Maggie.

Maggie whirled around and began staring into a glass case beneath the counter. Some strange-looking undergarments were displayed in a row.

"They're just for fun," explained the woman to Maggie. "Just, like, goofy—you know, a little gag gift for the guys . . ."

"Oh," said Maggie. She walked away and pretended to be interested in the terry cloth robes.

"Iris?"

Iris was examining a black lace nightie and some sort of see-through cape that went with it. And teeny-weeny undies! She peered at them. What good would they do as underpants?

"Iris?" said Maggie again. "Can you come here for a minute?"

Iris walked over.

Maggie picked up a sleeve of the robe and positioned herself between Iris and the woman. She mouthed the words: *Look—in—the—case.*

"At the wolf," she whispered out of the corner of her mouth. "And the giraffe!"

"Yes!" said Iris in a phony voice. "It is a nice robe!" She casually browsed her away across the store. She smiled at the woman behind the counter, who smiled back.

"Need help?" said the woman.

Iris shook her head no. Then she looked into the case at the assortment of animal-head underpants for men. "Nice shorts," said Iris.

"Shorts?"

"Or whatever they're called," said Iris.

Maggie winced.

"My mom bought my dad something similar to these. For their anniversary," volunteered Iris. "She showed them to me. But they were nowhere as good as these.

"They were going on a safari to photograph elephants . . ."

"Ah," said the woman.

". . . so my mom bought my dad a pair of elephant-head underpants. So he would kind of . . . blend in with the scenery."

Maggie hid.

"Ah," repeated the woman.

"Apparently that's all he wore. All over Kenya."

The woman looked at Iris, who shrugged. "It was very hot," said Iris, "at that time of year so

15

he just ran around in his skivvies. Maggie?"

Maggie froze.

"Where'd my friend go?" said Iris.

"I'm here," said Maggie. She stepped out from behind the rack of robes.

Iris smiled at her. "Anyway," she continued, "my mother said my father was looking up into the top of a bush at a bushtit—that's a bird, you know—with his binoculars and somebody almost shot him. An elephant poacher—an ivory poacher."

Maggie tried to keep from laughing, but a little squeak came out. "Can we get going?" she said, when Iris and the woman looked in her direction. "We told Mom we'd meet her in ten minutes." She looked at her watch. "It's already been six minutes!"

"Okay, but not until you see these underpants," said Iris.

"I saw them," said Maggie.

"Again!" said Iris. "Look at the wolf ones! Look at the beady little eyes! And the plastic teeth!"

With a sigh, Maggie walked over to the display case.

"And the whiskers! Look how hairy the nose is!"

"Great," said Maggie. She stepped on Iris's

foot as hard as she could. "Now can we go?"

They giggled all the way to Zone Music.

"Don't do anything at Zone Music," said Maggie. "I mean it." They went inside, where the clerk, a rocker with long hair, was fiddling with an electric guitar.

"Hey!" he said. "What's happening?"

"Hi," said Maggie. She lowered her eyelids halfway and looked at Iris. "I *mean* it," she whispered.

Iris said nothing. She waited politely while Maggie looked through the compact discs.

"Can you find what you're looking for?" said the guy. He played notes up the neck of the guitar—higher and higher—making a face as if he were in pain.

"She's looking for a Mister Rogers CD," said Iris. "Is Mister Rogers under the *M*'s?"

The guy looked puzzled.

"You know—Fred Rogers? The 'Won't You Be My Neighbor?' one?" said Iris.

Maggie sighed deeply. "I'm looking for the new Madonna CD."

"We're out," said the guy.

Iris turned toward the door. "Hurry up," she called to Maggie, "or you'll be late for your rumba lesson!"

TWO

Maggie's mother was standing outside the health food store, eating a sesame seed something. Dinah was beside her, sucking her thumb and twiddling her hair.

"Good," said Maggie's mother when Iris and Maggie walked up. "Ten minutes on the nose." She smiled at the girls. Then she opened the brown paper bag she was carrying and invited them to look into it.

"Carob chips?" said Maggie. "No, thanks, Mom. Really." She rolled her eyes at Iris. "They're, like, totally gross." She looked at her mother. "So now we can go to Marge's. Right?"

"Right," said Maggie's mother.

"Me too," said Dinah.

"By *ourselves!*" said Maggie.

"Calm down," said Maggie's mother. "You can go to Marge's by yourselves. We'll meet in fifteen minutes. In front, by the window. Okay?"

Both of the girls looked at Maggie's watch.

"And don't buy any tarantulas," said Maggie's mother.

Iris and Maggie headed off to Marge's Pet and Novelty Shop. "There's Marge," said Maggie, as they walked in.

A woman wearing denim overalls and a spoonbill cap was in the reptile room. She looked at them through the glass door and saluted. Maggie saluted back.

"What is this, the army?" mumbled Iris.

They began looking through things in the gag section: rubber barf, large and small elephant messes, chili pepper gum. "Just what happened last time," said Maggie. "She's out of invisible ink."

In the ADULTS ONLY, PLEASE! section, Iris peered into a small gray box and found a wind-up something inappropriate—that hopped. She wound it up.

"Don't," whispered Maggie. They watched it hippity hop across the counter and tip over.

"Gross," whispered Maggie. She looked up at Iris. "How much is it?"

"I'll ask," whispered Iris.

"No, you won't!"

Suddenly, they heard a yelp from the reptile room. They hurried to the door. Through the window they could see Marge making a horrible face; a hermit crab was hanging from her hand. "Ahh-ow!" she was yelling. *"Ow!"*

Cautiously, Maggie and Iris walked in. It was hot and stinky. Marge was peering at the palm of her hand. There were white quotation marks on it.

A small crab in a green shell was walking sideways across the floor.

"That's the worst I've ever been pinched," said Marge, without looking up. "And I've been in the business thirty years. Dang!" she added, shaking her head. She wiped her hand on the back of her pants, then looked at her palm again.

She stooped over and picked up the crab. "You double-doggone dash be-blinkered son-of-a-sidewinder," she said. "Whoa!" It dangled out of its shell, upside down, menacing Marge with its claw. "Look at this thing, will you? And they're supposed to be shy!" she said to Maggie, who stepped back.

But Iris moved closer.

"How much is it?" she asked.

"Three bucks," said Marge.

Iris dug into her jeans.

"But that's just the beginning, with these critters. They need a whole habitat. A plastic box and gravel," said Marge, "and crab chow and crab cakes. And a water dish—and something to climb on. And an extra shell. They change shells, hermit crabs."

Iris took out the twenty and the ten and neatly unfolded them.

Marge rubbed the palm of her hand with her thumb. "And consider a first-aid kit—and maybe a few butterfly bandages." She stared at Iris for a moment, and Iris stared back.

"You think I'm afraid of that crab?" said Iris.

Marge kept looking at Iris, but Iris didn't look away. Marge had to frown a little, to keep from smiling. "O-kay," she said, gruffly. "Whatever you say. But don't say I didn't warn you."

Iris followed Marge around the store. "Actually," Marge told her, "you can use jar lids for the dishes, instead of buying them. Crabs can climb on anything—a stick, any kind of a rock." Iris was eyeballing a twelve-dollar crystal sitting near some coral on the shelf. "Don't run your bill up. That's somebody's hard-earned dough you've got in your fist. You don't need that fancy crystal. Save the crystals for the airheads and the faith healers—they can use them to cure warts."

She walked away, whistling a tune she seemed to be making up as she went along. "And you saw firsthand how that thing pinches, so don't blame me," said Marge.

She shifted a few cardboard boxes around with her boot. "You're my witness," she said to Mag-

21

gie. "And tell your mother: I warned your friend. She saw for herself."

"I know," said Maggie. "I heard you."

"I'm not going to get pinched by the crab!" cried Iris.

"And tell your mother the neon tetras will be in the first of the week," said Marge to Maggie. "She called about them."

"Okay," said Maggie.

Iris shoveled some aquarium gravel into a bag, spilling it.

Marge shook a cigarette out of a package and tapped it on her thumbnail. "Kids," she mumbled. She lit the cigarette in the doorway and blew a few smoke rings.

"I thought you decided secondary smoke was bad for the lizards," said Maggie.

Marge shrugged. "Am I in the reptile room?"

Maggie poked through a basket of shells. "Get this purple one." She gave Iris the shell. "So she has something to grow into." She took Iris aside. "Please don't ask about the wind-up you-know-what," she whispered.

Marge looked over. "You need something else?"

Maggie froze.

"Just this shell," said Iris.

Maggie breathed a sigh of relief. She strolled

over to where Marge's huge red-and-yellow parrot was sitting on a perch. It began whistling the Oscar Mayer wiener song.

"Twenty-eight seventy-five," said Marge, after she'd written everything on a receipt pad and put the pencil behind her ear.

Iris handed her the money.

"Did you want anything, Maggie?" said Iris. "Wasn't there something you saw that—"

"No," said Maggie.

"Not that—"

"*No!*" said Maggie. "I don't want anything!"

"Okay," said Iris. "I was only asking."

"You hang on to her change," said Marge to the crab.

They walked out of the shop, Iris holding the plastic box with gravel in it—and a beautiful chunk of white crystal in the gravel and the crab clinging to the top of the crystal with a dollar clamped in its claw.

They waited in front of the shop window.

"What do you think I should name her?" said Iris.

"I don't know," said Maggie. "How about 'Goat Body'?"

Iris looked thoughtful.

"Or 'Ivy Lou.' I've always liked 'Ivy Lou' for a

crab. Or . . ." Maggie brightened. "Why not 'Iris'?" she said, cheerfully. "She acts like you!"

Iris said nothing.

"She's crabby like you. And she looks like you!" said Maggie.

Iris frowned.

"She does!" cried Maggie.

Maggie's mother walked up. "No. Don't tell me," she said. She put her hand on her forehead. Dinah looked into the plastic box.

"It isn't a tarantula," Iris said. "And I can get sneakers another time."

"And Mom?" said Maggie. "What do you think of the name 'Goat Body'?"

"How much was all this?"

"Or what about 'Ivy Lou'?" said Maggie. " 'Goat Body'? Or 'Ivy Lou'?"

"Hmmm," said Maggie's mother. She thought a minute. "Well, 'Goat Body' does have a nice kind of . . . ring to it," she said. She shaded her eyes and looked through the window at Marge, who made a don't-blame-it-on-me gesture.

"The neon tetras will be in the first of the week!" called Marge.

"I thought you quit smoking!" Maggie's mother called back.

"I said I was *going* to!" called Marge.

"Well . . . when, then?"

"When the cows come home!" called Marge.

Maggie's mother shook her fist at Marge, and they all walked away, Dinah hanging on to Iris's elbow.

"Does anybody need to stop in the women's room before we head home?" said Maggie's mother. "Dinah?"

Dinah didn't answer.

"Do you?"

"No."

"You're sure?"

"Yes!"

"Don't shout at me," said her mother.

"I like the name 'Mister Nibbles,' " said Dinah to Iris.

"You better not say you have to go to the bathroom as soon as we walk out of here," said Mrs. Hunter to Dinah.

In the car, Iris sat in the front beside Mrs. Hunter, carefully holding the plastic box on her lap.

"I have to go pee," said Dinah, as they pulled into Iris's driveway. "Quick!"

Everybody piled out of the car and hurried into the house. Iris waved Maggie into her bedroom and shut the door. She set the plastic box on the edge of her desktop and used it like a bull-dozer to clear a space. "Maggie," she said, "let me ask you something."

"What?"

"Would you or would you not *love* to see this crab hanging from the end of Corky Newton's nose?"

In the hall, Mrs. Fuller struck up a conversation with Maggie's mother. "Fridee I go to my sister Irene's. Then Satdee I stay, and Sundee I stay, and Mondee I'm home. And e-gads! She's making me take her to Marine World Fridee afternoon—it's Ladies' Day! Cuppa tea?"

"I'd love to," lied Maggie's mother, "but we really have to run."

"That Irene," said Mrs. Fuller. She shook her head, and Maggie's mother tried to look sympathetic—although she didn't quite know why.

"I'm thirsty," said Dinah.

"We really have to go," said her mother.

"Well, follow me," said Mrs. Fuller to Dinah.

"Just a little water will be fine," said Maggie's mother.

"So," said Mrs. Fuller. "Fridee morning the folks will come home." She closed her eyes for a minute. "And I te' ya, it's been a long trip. Six weeks to buy ladies' underpants. Six weeks!" She took a small glass from a shelf in the cupboard and poured Dinah something green from a plastic container in the refrigerator. "I te' ya." She gave the glass to Dinah and pointed to a chair.

"By the way," said Maggie's mother, in an apologetic way, "Iris bought a hermit crab and a . . . habitat in the pet store at the mall. I hope it's okay."

"And here I thought she was getting sneakers with the money, but oh so what," said Mrs. Fuller. "At least you can eat a crab. And at least it isn't a mule! She's been after me to buy her a mule she saw advertised in the paper."

"Land sakes," she added.

Maggie's mother sighed. "Ready, Dinah?"

"I'm hungry," said Dinah.

"Dinner's soon," said her mother.

Mrs. Fuller got a box of vanilla wafers down from the cupboard. "I love these," she said.

She rattled the box at Maggie's mother, who shook her head no. "Really. But thank you."

Mrs. Fuller handed the box to Dinah. "So," said Mrs. Fuller. "Iris was saying something about your ex getting married again. . . ."

"That's what I hear," said Maggie's mother, quietly.

"Man oh man!" said Mrs. Fuller. *"That* was quick." She eyed Maggie's mother. "Will the bride be wearing white?"

Maggie's mother changed the subject. "I wasn't even aware you had a sister," she said. "How long has she lived in the area?"

"Who, Irene?"

Dinah carefully added one more small round cookie to the tower of cookies she had constructed on the table in front of her. "Dinah?" said her mother. "One cookie. *One.*"

"Oh, let her have them," said Mrs. Fuller. "I've got plenty. I've got another box in the pantry. You just have as many as you please," Mrs. Fuller said to Dinah, and patted the top of her head. "You're as cute as a button. Here! Take the box!"

Maggie's mother sighed again, this time making a slight groaning sound.

"Them men," said Mrs. Fuller. "My husband left me for a waitress, but I guess I told you that. Years ago, when he was just out of the service."

"Maggie!" called her mother. "Please!"

"That dirty dog," said Mrs. Fuller.

Maggie appeared in the kitchen.

"Let's go, okay? Say good-bye to Iris. Dinah, say thank you to Mrs. Fuller."

"Why are you mad at *me?*" said Maggie.

"I'm not!" her mother answered. "Can we go, please? *Thank* you, Mrs. Fuller." She ushered Dinah and Maggie out of the kitchen. "Have a *wonderful* trip to Marine World!"

Iris came out of her room. "Thank you for taking me to the mall, Mrs. Hunter."

"And you know what?" said Mrs. Fuller. "After he left me for a waitress, he left that waitress for a trapeze lady in the circus—a ninety-five pounder! A real tramp. And you know what?"

Maggie's mother didn't answer.

"They both ended up getting sent up the river for bad checks. The both of 'em."

Iris tried to wave, but Mrs. Fuller was blocking the doorway. "But 'What goes around comes around' is what I always say," she called.

"What's she talking about?" whispered Maggie.

"Who knows?" whispered Maggie's mother. She smiled and waved.

"I don't know how Iris can stand it," Maggie's mother said as they backed out onto Locust Street. "I honestly don't!" She drove a couple of blocks. "That woman is intolerable. Intolerable!"

She pulled over and stopped by the park.

"I mean, everybody has a right to take a little trip—and it really isn't any of my business— but to leave a kid with Mrs. Fuller . . . for six weeks? What *could* her parents have been thinking?"

She got out of the car and pitched the box of vanilla wafers into the trash.

"Can I have a hermit crab sometime?" called Maggie.

THREE

*I*ris sat at the breakfast table, eating a bowl of Cocoa Puffs and chocolate milk—an excellent combination.

Mrs. Fuller was packing Iris's school lunch and, as usual, was in the mood to chat. "My sister Irene is bound and determined for me to get her to Marine World Fridee," she told Iris, "but holy smoke! To hike around that place!"

Iris began reading the back of the cereal box.

"And that Irene—she's put on a lot of bulk over the years. She's not the gal she used to be, no sir. In the old days," Mrs. Fuller continued, "Irene was slim. Oh yes! And tall! She was tall and slim, taller than the other girls. Then she fell off the roof and quit growing." She lowered her voice. "And I mean everywhere! She's still flat as a board, even with the weight gain."

Iris glanced up at her. "Your sister fell off a roof? And quit growing? When?"

"Oh, she didn't really fall off the roof. That's

31

the old-fashioned expression for starting the monthlies."

Iris closed her eyes and sighed.

"Yup! She started trottin' on cotton, and that was it for the boozoms—boozoms quit growing, you know, when the monthlies start. Along with everything else."

Boozoms? Monthlies? *Trottin' on cotton?*

"Except the feet. And Irene's got some gunboats on her, I te' ya. Anyway, back to the boozoms . . . She was very self-conscious, that Irene." Mrs. Fuller giggled. "The girls used to tease her in gym. They used to call her 'bee stings.' What's that joke again? 'When the Lord passed out the boozoms, she was standing behind the door!' And speaking of which—did I show you this?"

She shuffled her slippers across the linoleum. "This came yesterday, from your mother."

She handed Iris a postcard with a picture of a beautiful sculpture of a nude mother and child in marble. "Read it."

Iris turned it over.

"Dear Iris," it said in tiny writing.

> You won't believe what happened to me yesterday. Daddy was busy, so I went to

32

the Louvre museum. After seeing some of the exhibits, I went to the ladies' room downstairs, left the museum, walked across a long courtyard, stopped at an intersection and waited for the light to change, crossed the street, and went into a building where there was an American Express office.

"Um, eggs-kuse me," said a woman in line behind me, "but, um, your dress—it eez tucked into your pantee 'ose and everysing is showing.

"And I mean everysing!"

See you Friday.

Love,
Mom

Iris smiled a little. She turned the postcard over to look at the picture again.

"Pretty picture," said Mrs. Fuller, taking it from Iris. "Too bad one of 'em's arms is broken off." She set the card on the windowsill. Then she rolled Iris's lunch bag closed at the top and tapped her watch. "Now scram."

Iris stuffed the lunch bag into her pack. Where was her *Aesop's Fables*? Oh, well. She could borrow somebody's.

She left the house and walked along the sidewalk toward Pengrove Junior High. A couple of eighth-grade boys were ahead of her. One pushed the other into a bush.

Iris was the last person into her homeroom. Mrs. Gersen arched an eyebrow. "We were just collecting the pledge envelopes for the music department. . . ."

"My mom and dad still aren't home yet," said Iris.

"Oh," said Mrs. Gersen. "Right. I forgot. They're in England or something. On a business trip?"

"France," said Iris.

Mrs. Gersen read announcements. The bell rang. Most of the kids left the class, but Iris and a few of the others stayed seated, since Mrs. Gersen was their first-period English teacher.

The vice-principal, Mr. Kennedy, walked in, carrying a clipboard.

"Good morning!" said Mrs. Gersen.

"Good morning," said Mr. Kennedy.

Corky Newton burst into the room. "Mrs. Gersen?" he said. "Are you going to love this! Are you *ever* going to love this—"

"Can you hang on a minute, Corky?" said Mrs. Gersen. "I'm talking with Mr. Kennedy—"

"My uncle gave me a hand puppet—from

Europe, you know? It's all hand carved. You wouldn't believe it. . . ."

Mrs. Gersen and Mr. Kennedy were looking at a list on the clipboard.

"It's a little boy," continued Corky, "wearing lederhosen. You know, those little gray leather shorts with suspenders attached? And he has a little, tiny Alpine hat, a felt one. And a little carved face. He cost two hundred dollars!" Corky looked around the room at the faces of the kids who had wandered in.

"Big deal," mumbled Iris.

"And my parents said we could use it in the puppet show—as long as I didn't let anybody else touch it."

Iris turned around and stared at him.

"Especially not *her*," he said, pointing to Iris. "It cost two hundred dollars! Do you think I'm kidding? It's an antique!" he added.

"That would be very nice," said Mrs. Gersen. "We'd like to see the puppet very much."

"We would?" mumbled Iris. She yawned.

"However," said Mrs. Gersen slowly, "I'm not sure we'll need to use the puppet in the performance. After all, the point of the puppet show is to do it ourselves. It's a creative endeavor, Corky—"

"But—"

"And I was hoping all of you would make puppets from scratch. You know, we discussed this—using this and that from around your house. Buttons and string. And yarn and socks and—"

"Listen!" cried Corky. "He even has a little pin on his hat made of sterling silver—an ice ax—with a white flower on it."

"I'm sure it's unique," said Mrs. Gersen. "But the main idea of the show is to make your *own* puppets and participate in the scriptwriting—from *Aesop's Fables*—and make the puppet stage."

"Please!" said Corky. "You should see it! It's not fair to make people make puppets if they already have one they want to use!"

Mrs. Gersen sighed loudly. "Well, what fable?" she said, in an impatient way. "What fable? What character would this puppet represent?"

Iris spoke without raising her hand. "Isn't there a little boy in the fable about the ass?" she said in a loud voice. "I would think Corky would be excellent in that one."

A few of the students exchanged glances.
Somebody laughed.

" 'The Ass and the Horse'?" said Mrs. Gersen. "I don't think there's a boy in 'The Ass and the

Horse.' " She looked at Arthur Frisco, who was head of the Scriptwriting and Fable Selection Committee.

"No," said Arthur Frisco. "There isn't a boy in 'The Ass and the Horse.' " He pretended to be puzzled. Then he rested his hand on his forehead, as though he was thinking very hard.

The room grew quiet.

"But," said Arthur, raising his eyebrows, "there *is* one in 'The Boy Who Cried Wolf.' "

"Yes," said Mrs. Gersen. "I suppose that's an idea. . . ." She looked thoughtful. "But do we have a wolf? I know Gina's making the fox for 'The Fox and the Grapes,' but—"

"I'll make the wolf," said Iris.

Mrs. Gersen turned to her.

"You'll make the wolf? I thought you said you didn't want to make a puppet."

"Suddenly, I've changed my mind," said Iris.

Mrs. Gersen stared at her.

"Really. I've changed my mind, and I have a sudden burning need to make a puppet." She paused. "The wolf rips the boy's head off, doesn't it?"

"Well, I don't know about that. . . ."

"But it does kill the boy—some way or another," said Iris.

"Yes," said Mrs. Gersen.

Iris turned around and looked at Corky. "Then I'll make the wolf," she said.

"Okay," said Mrs. Gersen. "Settled. Iris will make the wolf."

Corky Newton groaned.

Mrs. Gersen ignored him. "But can you finish it by Monday?" she asked Iris. "You're really getting a late start. And you were supposed to be on the Scriptwriting and Fable Selection Committee, weren't you?"

"I can live without her," said Arthur.

"No, you can't," said Iris to Arthur, with a frown.

"Well, what about the script for 'The Boy Who Cried Wolf'?" said Mrs. Gersen. "Will there be time to get that done at this late date?"

"I'll write the script," said Iris. "Put me down for it, will you, Art? I'll work on it in the library at lunch and finish it tonight for homework."

She continued to frown at Arthur, who frowned at her.

"*And* I'll write any other script Art wants me to—"

"My name is Arthur," said Arthur to Iris.

"*And,*" said Iris, making a face at him before turning to Mrs. Gersen, "I'll finish the puppet by Monday. My mom and dad are coming home. They can help me over the weekend."

"Will you have time to take on this additional editing work?" Mrs. Gersen asked Arthur.

"Does she know the scriptwriting format?"

"Yes," said Iris.

"Well, I suppose," said Arthur.

"O-kay . . ." Mrs. Gersen sighed. She walked up close to Iris. "But no shenanigans."

Iris looked innocent.

"I mean it!" said Mrs. Gersen. "You and Corky have had a certain amount of difficulty getting along these first few weeks. . . ."

"First few weeks?" mumbled Arthur. "Try 'last few years'!"

"It will work out," said Iris. "Really." She looked at Corky Newton.

And smiled a wicked little smile.

Mrs. Gersen walked over to the chart hanging on the wall and wrote "Corky—Boy Who Cried Wolf" and "Iris—Wolf" under the PUPPETS column and "Iris—Boy Who Cried Wolf" under the SCRIPTWRITERS column. "Now what else?" she said, looking up at the class. "William? Didn't you say you were making the stag?"

"I did," said William. "But I gave up. I didn't have any yarn for the mane. And I couldn't paint the carrots with brown paint for the antlers."

Iris leaned close to Stella, who was sitting across the aisle. "A deer with a mane?" she whispered. "This guy is unbelievable."

"And I couldn't glue the carrots to the sock, either," said William. "And my father wants to know why we're doing art in English class."

"Carrots to the sock?" said Mrs. Gersen. "Look," she said. "Get a grip, okay, William? We already went through all of this. And you can tell your father that if he has any questions about the program, my number's in the book.

"Just bring a sock to school. You can go through the button tin for eyes, and you can cut a felt tongue. There's felt in the scrap bag, and there's yarn for a tail. Isn't there?" She looked at Arthur.

"Yes," said Arthur. "But he'll just have to figure out the antlers—"

"He can cut a hole in the top of the head and poke his fingers through for the antlers," said a girl in the back row.

"Oh, right!" said Corky sarcastically.

"Actually," said Mrs. Gersen, "that's a rather clever idea. As I said earlier, I encourage all of you to be imaginative and creative in your concepts for puppet making. It's a good solution:

William can poke his fingers through the holes and hold them like antlers."

"And he could wrap them with tinfoil," added Iris, "and shape it like antlers."

Corky laughed out loud. Mrs. Gersen stared at him. "Sorry," said Corky. "It's just that . . . Never mind.

"It's a totally stupid idea!" he whispered loudly to the boy sitting next to him.

Mrs. Gersen cleared her throat. "Corky?"

She waited until Corky Newton looked at her. "The vice-principal has kindly volunteered to clear the display case in the hallway outside the office so that a few of us can display our puppets after the show—for open house."

Corky raised his hand and asked, "Will the few that are picked be covered by insurance?"

FOUR

*I*ris slammed the door. "Mrs. Fuller!" she called.

Mrs. Fuller had just plopped down in an easy chair when Iris rushed into the den.

"Listen!" said Iris. "We have to go to the mall. Now!"

"I just sat down!" said Mrs. Fuller.

"It's an emergency," said Iris. "I have to go to Bernadette's. I need wolf-head underpants—for men."

"Wolf-head what?"

"Underpants! To sew onto a sock. And stuff the nose for a puppet—they're in Bernadette's. And there's only one pair left. It's an assignment!"

"An assignment?"

"For English. And I need to pick up my film. For art! Or I'll get an F!"

"Why would anybody need wolf-nose underpants for a puppet?" said Mrs. Fuller. "Why would anybody need wolf-nose underpants for *anything*?"

"Wolf-*head!*" said Iris.

"Wolf-anything!" cried Mrs. Fuller. "Wolf-anything underpants for a puppet! I've never heard of such a thing!"

Iris looked calmly at Mrs. Fuller. "Look," she said. "When's the last time you made a puppet?"

Mrs. Fuller appeared thoughtful. "I don't know as I've ever made a puppet. I made dolls out of clothespins when I was a little girl, out of little wooden clothespins and scraps of material from my mother's sewing basket, but—"

"I'm telling you: Everybody makes puppets out of underpants these days. Why freak over a pair of undies—they're just a piece of cloth! Even Maggie's mother makes stuffed animals and things out of underpants—they're making a goose and sending it to Maggie's grandfather. And Maggie's mother's an artist, so she knows what she's talking about, and she said I should do it—that I should be creative—and my teacher said we had to be 'imaginative and creative in our concepts for puppet making.' "

"Well, how do we pay? We've already run through practically all the cash your mother left—what with that hermit crab!"

"Ivy Lou? She only cost three dollars!"

"Yes. But the plastic box—how much was that? And the purple shell? And the crab chow? And the crab cakes?"

"You don't want her to eat?"

"Yes, I want her to eat. But what about the crystal?"

"Hermit crabs are supposed to climb," said Iris.

"On a twelve-dollar crystal?" said Mrs. Fuller.

"She's worth it. Exercise is important to everybody. So, everybody up! Come on, up you get! You're worse than your sister Irene!"

Mrs. Fuller frowned at Iris.

"We can charge the underpants," said Iris.

"On what card?" cried Mrs. Fuller.

"Well, you have cash, don't you?"

Mrs. Fuller sighed. "Yes, I have cash."

"And Mom always reimburses you in an emergency. . . ."

"Wolf-head underpants is an emergency?" said Mrs. Fuller. She closed her eyes and shook her head. "My sainted aunt."

"Oh, come on," said Iris, gently. She picked up Mrs. Fuller's hand and patted it. "You need the exercise—look at you!"

"What do you mean, look at me!"

"I'll get your purse," said Iris.

She ran into the kitchen and grabbed Mrs.

Fuller's beige plastic purse from the table. "I'll drive!" she shouted, as she raced outside.

Mrs. Fuller jumped up and hurried after her. When she got to the car, Iris was sitting behind the wheel. "I'll have a cheeseburger," she said to Mrs. Fuller. "Hold the mustard. And some fries."

Mrs. Fuller waved her hand and said, "Scoot over! But if you think I'm going into a store with you to buy men's wolf-hair underpants for a puppet, you're mistaken." They backed out of the driveway, onto the street. "Maggie Hunter's mother may do it, but what would you expect? Some of these artists paint pictures that show everything. And I mean everything! No sir! No siree bob!"

Iris said nothing.

"I'm going to wait outside."

Mrs. Fuller glanced at Iris.

Iris looked out the window.

"I'm going to wait outside the store and you go in," said Mrs. Fuller. "I'm not an artist. I'm just a plain, ordinary old lady who does certain things a certain way. I've never had my own children, but I know enough to know that underpants do not belong in school under any circumstances."

Iris switched on the radio and spun the knob

until she found a rock station. She turned up the volume.

An elderly gentleman, dapper in a gray felt hat, was walking along the sidewalk bordering the park. Iris rolled down her window as they approached. "Go slow," she said to Mrs. Fuller. "I think I know this guy."

Mrs. Fuller put on the brake.

"Pull over a little closer," said Iris. She turned down the radio. "I want to say hello."

Mrs. Fuller rolled slowly by him. But just as they were passing, Iris ducked her head and blasted the horn. She began frantically waving her arm near the steering wheel, so that it looked as if Mrs. Fuller was greeting the man.

Mrs. Fuller stepped on the gas and quickly drove away. She checked the rearview mirror; the man was standing on the sidewalk, smiling and waving his cane.

"What a lousy trick," said Mrs. Fuller.

"Yes!" cried Iris. "Yes!" She turned up the radio. "Hammer!" She closed her eyes. "I *have* to get his new tape." She slumped in her seat and poked her chin in and out to the music until they got to the mall.

Mrs. Fuller parked, and they walked inside. They passed the shoe store, and a young man in a suit waved to Iris.

He came to the doorway. "My favorite cus-tomer!" he said to Iris, with a grin. "We've got some new high-tops in; right up your alley!" He pointed to a pair of sneakers in the window. "Take a look!" They were printed with reptile designs. "There's even a rattlesnake here!"

"I know. I saw them yesterday," said Iris. "We'll come back by and get them."

"We will?" muttered Mrs. Fuller under her breath.

The man winked at Iris, and she waved.

"He's nice," Iris said to Mrs. Fuller, who was walking along with a scowl on her face. "He's the one who sold me my green sparkly flats."

"Underpants and sneakers, and then that's it," said Mrs. Fuller. "And don't ask for anything else."

"I won't. But you know what? Dad said if I go out for basketball he'll take me to The Athlete's Foot when he gets home and get me some Nike Airs."

Mrs. Fuller stopped and looked in a gift shop window.

"Or Reebok Pumps," said Iris.

"In' that adorable?" said Mrs. Fuller. "Why don't you ever buy something cute, like that?" She pointed to an ashtray made out of two kiss-ing frogs. "Now, *that* would make a nice puppet if you put it on a table and hid under the table to do your talking."

"Let's get going," said Iris. She took Mrs. Fuller's arm.

"No sir," said Mrs. Fuller, when they reached Bernadette's. "I'm not going in there. I said it, and I mean it: I will not shop for men's wolf underpants." With a sigh, she plunked down on a wooden bench.

Iris walked into the store and made a beeline for the counter.

"Hello," said the woman.

"Good!" cried Iris. "They're still here!" She tapped on the glass. "I need the wolf-heads."

The woman looked at her.

"For my brother," said Iris. She stared through the glass at the flimsy satin underpants. "He's moving to the Yukon."

The woman softly bit her mouth and lowered an eyelid. "Hmmm. Let me ask you something. . . ."

Iris waited.

"It's cold in Alaska. Have you considered something more along the lines of, say, flannel long johns? I bought my nephew some long johns at Mervyn's a couple of years ago. Does your brother wear long johns?"

Iris looked up at her. "He did when he was two."

The woman said nothing.

"Now he likes wolves," said Iris. She tapped again on the glass above the underpants. "He's going to dedicate his life to studying wolves."

"O-kay," said the woman. "But I don't really think the manufacturer had them in mind for the Yukon. . . ."

"Nobody has anything in mind for the Yukon," said Iris. "Nobody cares about the wolves anymore." She shook her head. "They're endangered, you know."

The woman looked at Iris with a concerned expression.

"Thank God for people like my brother," said Iris.

The woman agreed. She leaned down and pulled out the underpants by their long whiskered nose and held them in the air.

"These *are* sweet," she said, laying them carefully on the counter. "Aren't they? And why shouldn't the guys have the chance to wear cute underpants? They're harmless enough."

Iris said nothing.

"You know, they growl when you pinch the nose," said the woman.

They *did?* Iris was elated.

"But like I said, they won't be that warm," said the woman. She turned them around; there were just a couple of flimsy elastic strings in the back to hold them up. "So I'm not making any guarantees about how cozy they'd be for wolfing."

"I'll take them," said Iris, after reading a tiny white tag attached to the elastic that said $15.95.

And pinching the nose.

"But before you wrap them up . . ." Iris leaned a little closer to the woman and said, in a soft voice, "Remember that girl I was in here with? She asked me to pick out a padded bra for her—she's shy."

"How padded?"

"Majorly," said Iris. "Like, *big.*" She held her hands a considerable distance from the front of her chest.

"Uh-huh," said the woman.

"She's been waiting for Mother Nature to . . . fill her out, *if* you know what I mean. But she's going to be a junior bridesmaid in a wedding in March, and when she tried on the dress . . . Well, let's just say she needs help. Fast."

"What size bra does your . . . friend wear?"

"Small," said Iris. She looked down at her

chest. "She wears a thirty-four A—but my guess is that it's probably half empty."

"Well, if you'll follow me . . . ," said the woman.

Iris followed her over to a round rack with bras of all colors hanging from it. They looked like life preservers.

The woman took one from its see-through plastic hanger and pinched the cups. "This ought to do you," she said. She handed it to Iris.

Iris took it and pinched the cups.

"Listen," said the woman. "Why don't you try it on . . . for your friend. You look like you're about a thirty-four A—and if it fits you, maybe it will fit her." She smiled at Iris. "And if it doesn't, maybe you can wear it."

At that moment, a dark and handsome brown-eyed boy walked into the store, followed by a distinguished-looking man in a three-piece suit.

Good grief! They were Iris's new neighbors!

"I'm looking for a robe for my wife," said the man. He had a Spanish accent. "Something warm." His son lingered in the doorway. "The movers lost a wardrobe box. . . ."

The woman smiled enthusiastically. "Well,

you've come to the right place!" she called. "Be right with you!"

The boy looked at Iris. Did he recognize her?

Iris quickly threw the bra onto the rack but it fell to the floor. Oops! She stepped on it! And trampled it! And the strap somehow got caught around her ankle. She tried to kick it off, but it wouldn't kick off. She had to lean down and extricate herself, and in stepping out of it, she left a large shoe mark on one of the cups.

"It will brush off," said the woman. She held the bra up to the light and whacked it a few times as Iris headed for the door.

"What about these?" the woman cried. She ran to the counter and waved the wolf-head underpants at Iris.

But Iris squeezed past the man and his son without answering and hurried out of the store.

"Brother!" she said when she reached Mrs. Fuller. "Now they let guys in the lingerie store." She glanced over her shoulder.

The boy was leaning against the doorjamb, gazing in her direction.

Iris's heart fluttered. "Let's get going!" she said, taking Mrs. Fuller's hand and pulling her off the bench. "Hurry up!"

"Where are the puppet pants?"

"Never mind!" cried Iris.

"Where are the wolf-skin underpants with a nose on the front?" said Mrs. Fuller in a loud voice.

"What are you talking about, 'wolf-skin'?" said Iris, making a face at Mrs. Fuller. She glanced sideways at the boy. "I don't need anything wolf-skin. I need rattlesnake-skin high-tops! At Sweet Feet—before they close the store!"

"I thought you said you needed men's under-pants!" Mrs. Fuller adjusted her glasses and stared at the boy. "Don't we know him?"

"Shhh!" whispered Iris. "No!"

Mrs. Fuller threw up her arms. "She drags me all the way down here for underpants," she called in the boy's direction, "and now she wants sneakers!"

"Come *on!*" moaned Iris. "I also need to go to Cameras and Moore!"

FIVE

The phone rang.

Iris leaned over and painted her pinkie toenail.

The phone rang again.

"Can you get it?" she called to Mrs. Fuller.

It rang again.

"Brother!" said Iris in a loud voice. She walked on her heels to the hall and answered the telephone.

"Sweetheart?" said her mother's voice from far away. "Hello?"

"Mom!" said Iris. "Where are you?"

"Still in Paris," said her mother. "Listen—we're going to be delayed."

Iris said nothing.

"Hello?"

"What do you mean, 'delayed'?" said Iris.

"We won't be home on Friday; we've changed our flight. We'll be home Saturday morning—"

"But I want you to come home on Friday!"

"We can't!"

"I've been waiting and waiting for you to come! I have something to tell you . . . some news."

"Well, what is it?"

"I don't want to say . . . on the phone." Iris lowered her voice to a whisper. "The operator might be listening."

"What?"

"Somebody might be listening!" said Iris.

"Nobody is listening."

"Well," said Iris. She paused.

Her mother sighed.

"Can you hear me?" whispered Iris.

"Barely!" said her mother. "What is it?"

"I started my period on Sunday!" whispered Iris.

"What?"

"My period!" whispered Iris.

"Mike who? I can't hear you!"

There was a bump in the kitchen; Iris thought she heard Mrs. Fuller coming. "Never mind," she said. "I'll tell you in person."

"Okay. Then tell me in person," said her mother. "I'm not going to play games with you, and I am *not* going to argue about when we are coming home. I'm sorry, but we *cannot* be home by Friday. Daddy had second thoughts about his selection of teddies and panties for the New York store, and we've got to choose a new line of slips for spring. There were problems with the silk—you know the lingerie business, honey. And Daddy has to change some shipping arrangements. It's one headache after another. . . ."

Iris was silent.

"Sweetheart? Are you there?"

"I wanted you to come home when you said! I need you to help me. I don't understand math anymore! I don't understand ratios, and I'm having a quiz!"

"Calm down. I'll help you on Saturday afternoon. There's nothing I'd rather do—really—than solve seventh-grade math problems. After spending sixteen hours on an airplane."

Tears sprang into Iris's eyes. She brushed them away. "Anyway," she said in a quiet voice, "what about Maggie and me? Did you get us the big balloony pants for the band?"

"Absolutely not," said her mother. "Balloony pants are *out!* Totally out! All the girls are wearing miniskirts over here. And stockings, with lace floral patterns. So I got you and Maggie each a black miniskirt and a pair of lace stockings patterned with violets and studded with the tiniest little rhinestones you've ever seen—they look like raindrops. And I got each of you—hang on to your hat—a real snakeskin garter belt, dyed neon green!"

"Why?" cried Iris.

"To hold up the stockings," said her mother.

"Why would they kill a snake for a garter belt?"

"Oh, please, Iris. They're all the rage again, even for preteens. Garter belts are making an absolute comeback; isn't that a riot? Garter belts! Anyway, trust me: You and Maggie are going to look so hot in your miniskirts and twinkly stockings from Paris you'll have to carry along a fire extinguisher. And if you and Maggie are afraid of going to Ecology Hell over the garter belts, I'll send them to your cousins in L.A. Have you and Maggie been practicing? Never mind! Tell me later. This phone call's costing a dollar a minute! Have you got a pencil? Find a pencil and a piece of paper—and get Mrs. Fuller, would you?"

Iris dropped the phone receiver onto the rug. Rats!

She'd been counting on her mom and dad being home on Friday; she was missing and missing them. And so much had happened since they'd been gone. There wasn't anyone to tell the news to about starting her period. She'd been lying to Maggie and the other girls about her period ever since fifth grade, when she'd gotten ketchup on her shorts after sitting on a hamburger at a Girl Scout barbecue.

Iris went into her room and tugged open her desk drawer; she rummaged through it until she found a broken crayon.

Her mother wasn't even going to come home when she promised.

She slammed the drawer.

She'd tell her mother if and when she ever *actually* made it home. *If* her mother was lucky. Iris tore a sheet of paper from her notebook and hurried out of her bedroom.

Mrs. Fuller was standing in the hall. "Somebody knocked the phone off the hook," she said. She yanked the receiver up by the cord and replaced it in its holder, then dusted the table with the feather duster she was holding.

Iris stared at her. "You just hung up on Mom."

"I did?"

"Mmm-hmm."

"That was stupid of me," said Mrs. Fuller.

Iris was inclined to agree. But she didn't see any reason to make Mrs. Fuller feel any worse than she already did. Iris felt a little sorry for Mrs. Fuller—she was such a dope.

"Don't worry about it," Iris told her. "Mom will call back."

"You think?" said Mrs. Fuller.

Iris nodded.

"Well, why do you suppose she called?" said Mrs. Fuller. "I hope everything's okay! Is the flight still coming in on time? She didn't say there was a problem with the airplane, did she?"

She put her hand on her throat.

Iris thought a moment before she answered.

"No," she said. "Nobody said anything about . . . problems with the airplane."

"Good," said Mrs. Fuller. "Otherwise, I'd have to tell Irene."

Iris began to hum a little tune.

"And that Irene! She really has been hounding me to come!" said Mrs. Fuller.

Iris grew very quiet. Maybe she should think this situation out. Her parents were going to be only one day late. What would be the point in having Mrs. Fuller baby-sit an extra day?

Iris bit her bottom lip. And thought a minute more. She couldn't think of a single good reason to tell Mrs. Fuller that her parents were going to be delayed.

If she did, Mrs. Fuller would have to cancel her plans to go to Marine World with Irene— and Irene was depending on her. *Depending* on her!

Besides, Irene needed to get up off her rear

end and take a hike around Marine World—all that sitting is bad for the circulation. Iris could easily stay one night without Mrs. Fuller. Her mother wouldn't care. If she did care, she'd be coming home Friday, as planned.

"She said everything's fine," said Iris. "She said, 'Have fun with Irene. And don't worry about anything.' "

"Well, I wish I hadn't hung up the darn phone!" said Mrs. Fuller. She stared at Iris.

Iris shrugged. "Well, what can you do?" she said. "Don't worry about it."

"Well, I just hope she calls back. If there's a problem or something—"

"There isn't a problem!" cried Iris.

"Well, maybe I shouldn't have told Irene I'd come in the first place. I hate to see your folks come home to an empty house, what with you at school and me gone to Vallejo. But it's Ladies' Day at Marine World—"

"Oh, come on now," said Iris. "Of course you should have told Irene you'd come. You never go visit Irene. . . ."

Mrs. Fuller put her fists on her hips and looked at Iris. "Well, when the heck does Irene visit me?"

Iris shrugged. How would she know when Irene visited Mrs. Fuller?

"Well, yes. Yes—I'll go visit Irene in Vallejo. But I te' ya, my circulation would be shot, too, if I sat around all day. You don't find me sitting around all day long, do you?

"No sir," said Mrs. Fuller before Iris had a chance to answer. "You don't find me sitting, that's for sure. I'll sweep the porch, but I won't sit on the porch, like that Irene. Sit on the porch and watch the grass grow . . .

"I'd rather sweep the porch and have the place shipshape for your parents than sit on my fat behind like Irene. And shouldn't the place be shipshape for your parents? They've been gone so long. . . ."

Iris said nothing.

But yes. They had been gone a long time. And Iris had completely grown up while her parents were gallivanting around Europe without her. Why should she even think twice about spending one night alone? She was a woman now. And since she was a woman, she was old enough to take care of herself. She didn't need a baby-sitter.

Mrs. Fuller had covered her finger with a flowered handkerchief and was poking it into one nostril and wiggling it around.

Ick!

Iris definitely, *definitely* did not need a baby-sitter for an extra night—she needed a break from the baby-sitter.

She would be fine for one afternoon and one evening. The silent alarm system worked perfectly well; Iris knew this, since she had accidentally triggered it by opening a window in the middle of the night, trying to lure in an owl with a piece of raw hamburger. Didn't the police come right over?

Plus, there were plenty of neighbors around, including a nice new family right next door. Iris looked at herself in the mirror above the hat stand. Certainly her parents would expect that a girl who'd started her period would be old enough to spend a few hours without a baby-sitter.

She turned sideways and glanced over her shoulder at herself and batted her eyelids. She was old enough to spend time without a baby-sitter, and she was old enough to wear a little mascara. Was there mascara upstairs in her mother's dressing table? "Have you seen any mascara in Mom's room?" she asked.

"Mascara?" said Mrs. Fuller. "No! And stay out of your mother's cosmetics. Please!"

Iris stared at Mrs. Fuller.

"I mean it!" said Mrs. Fuller. "And I noticed you've been rattling around in the cabinet under your mother's bathroom sink! That's ladies' business under there!" She bent over to pick up some trash Iris had pitched into the bottom of the umbrella stand, and she made a noise like somebody stepping on a whoopie cushion.

"I shouldn't eat cabbage," said Mrs. Fuller. "And this is *not* a garbage can!"

Iris gazed at herself in the mirror again. Yes. She could live very well without Mrs. Fuller for one night, because she could live very well without Mrs. Fuller for the rest of her life.

What right did Mrs. Fuller have to tell her to stay out of her mother's bathroom cabinet? She needed Stayfree maxipads, which—no thanks to Mrs. Fuller or anybody else—she had learned how to use. Of course, it *would* have been nice if her mother had been home to tell her which way was up on a maxipad; she had some uncomfortable moments before she figured out that the sticky stuff was supposed to stick to her underpants—not to her.

The phone rang, and Iris dove for it. "Hello? Just a minute. . . ." She covered the receiver. "It's my boyfriend," she whispered to Mrs. Fuller. "Do you mind if we . . . talk?"

"Well, don't talk long," said Mrs. Fuller. "Maybe your mother is trying to call back." She shook her head as she walked down the hallway. "Girls in the seventh grade with boyfriends!" she mumbled. "What next!" She took a broom from the closet and walked out the front door.

"Hi, Mom," said Iris quietly. "Sorry we got disconnected."

"It's this stupid French phone system," said her mother. "I can't believe it. Got the pencil?"

"Yup." Iris squeezed the receiver against her shoulder and held the paper against the wall.

"It's American Airlines, flight 802, arriving San Francisco at . . . let's see . . . eight-ten A.M. Eight-ten A.M. this Saturday, November sixteenth."

Iris wrote while her mother talked.

"Let me talk to Mrs. Fuller," said her mother.

"Mrs. Fuller?" Iris paused. She covered her eyes. "I can't see her. She went outside, but I can't see where she went."

The phone made some clicking noises.

"Can you hear me?" said Iris's mother.

"Sort of," said Iris. "But you sound like you're talking inside a barrel."

"Then help!" said her mother. "The operator's probably just about to disconnect us again. Never mind Mrs. Fuller. Just tell her not to leave on Friday morning; she'll have to stay an extra day. Tell her Daddy and I are checking out of this hotel in an hour or so, and we'll be on the road all day. Then we'll be on the plane, and we'll see you both on Saturday."

"No problem," said Iris.

"Well, don't forget to tell her. Did you write it down? Eight-ten Saturday morning? American Airlines?"

"Yes," said Iris. "Flight 802."

"But whatever you do, remember to tell her: we're hiring a limo—just like we originally planned. Daddy *cannot* handle being cooped up in a car with Mrs. Fuller. You know he can't stand the way she goes on and on—"

"I know," said Iris.

"You know he can't stand to be around her—"

"I said I know," said Iris.

"Besides, the limo driver can deal with the bags," said Iris's mother. "Daddy's had it with the bags! He wrenched his back—and blamed it on me. I've done a *lot* of shopping. . . ."

"Okay!" said Iris. Mrs. Fuller had finished sweeping and began shaking the mat.

"Well, I'll blow you a kiss!" said her mother. She blew a kiss to Iris.

Iris loudly blew a long kiss back into the receiver just as Mrs. Fuller walked back through the doorway. "I love you!" she said, dramatically.

"Be good!" said her mother. "I love you too!"

Iris hung up the phone. "He's such a doll," she whispered to Mrs. Fuller, with a sigh. Then she did some exaggerated dance steps down the hall and into her room, waving the paper in the air.

SIX

Iris stopped at her locker and waited while Cindi fiddled with her combination lock.

"I hate you!" said Cindi to the lock. She whirled it around and around again. Then she banged on the locker with her fist, and the door flew open. She stooped down and looked at herself in the mirror that was hanging inside.

"That shurt's fresh," Cindi told Iris. "Rully." She found some pink lipstick and put it on. "It's rully, like, totally . . ." She carefully pressed her lips together.

"Thanks," said Iris. She pulled her lunch bag out of the bottom of her pack and stared at it. There was a large grease spot on the bottom.

"Ick!" said Iris.

Cindi jumped up and waved some air past her nose with her hand. She faked a cough. "I mean, like, gag . . ." She rolled her eyes.

"Sardines again," said Iris. She salvaged a little package of Fun Fruits from the bag, while Cindi looked on in horror.

"Do you need to borrow some money for, like, a bagel dog or something?" said Cindi. "At the snack bar?"

"No, thanks," said Iris. "I hate bagel dogs. But thanks." She paused. "Did you know they put pig guts in bagel dogs?"

Cindi made a shocked face. "Are you surious?" She closed her eyes. "I did *not* hear you say that. . . ." She opened her eyes. "Hieee!" she squealed to somebody.

"Thure's Jake," she whispered to Iris, without moving her mouth.

"Hieee!" she squealed again.

A boy in a jaunty-looking hat smiled a crooked little smile at Cindi. "Hold me up!" she whispered to Iris. "Isn't he to *die* for?"

Cindi quickly untied her shoelace and hurried down the hallway in her purple-and-yellow cheerleader's outfit to where Jake was opening his locker.

She stopped next to him to tie her shoe.

Iris stuffed her pack into her locker and headed down the hall. She crossed the courtyard; a few kids were strolling around, talking and laughing, but almost everybody was inside, eating lunch. The custodian was watering the potted palms.

Iris walked into the lunchroom and looked

around for a place to sit. Unfortunately, she caught Corky Newton's eye. He opened his mouth and showed her the bagel dog he was chewing.

Corky Newton—what a slime ball.

Iris turned her head away.

She saw Stella and Jennifer. Iris sat down beside them and listened to Stella gripe about Walt Lacey. Stella was sure Walt liked her; at the dance two weeks earlier, he and Patrick Callagy had thrown cookies at her. Stella took a bite of her sandwich, and a slice of tomato fell out and landed on her chest.

Iris watched her carefully lift it off.

Brother.

Stella would certainly *not* be a candidate for The Flat People's Club.

Iris opened her package of Fun Fruits. What on earth could be fun about Fun Fruits? She shook a few of the sticky little orange blobs into her hand and stared at them. She wondered again about what Mrs. Fuller had told her. Once you started your period, did you really stop growing . . . everywhere? Iris hoped not!

"Boy, I'll be glad when my mom gets home," she said to Jennifer.

"Me too," said Jennifer. She handed Iris a stick of celery filled with peanut butter. "You've been eating my lunch ever since school started." She turned to Stella. "Did you know I actually have started packing extra stuff for her?"

"Are the Cool Ranch chips mine?" said Iris.

"No," said Jennifer.

"Ex-key-use *me!*" said a voice behind them. Corky Newton had circled around behind Iris and pretended to trip, shoving his bagel dog into Iris's back. "Oh, I'm *sorry!*" lied Corky Newton, in a loud voice. "I'm just so, *so* sorry!"

Iris shoved him backward into some chairs.

"Ouch!" moaned Corky. "Don't push!"

"Ick!" shouted Jennifer.

Stella jumped up. "Get away from us!"

The lunch supervisor turned to see what was happening.

"Hey, don't push!" cried Corky. "It was an accident!"

"I had an accident with this stuff," he said to the supervisor, in an innocent voice. He gooped some mustard off his bagel dog onto his finger and held it in the air. "I hope it doesn't stain!"

"Well, darlin', it does stain!" said the supervisor, in a Texas accent. "A course it stains!" She made a sympathetic face at Iris. "In' that a shame? What a mayess!" She reached for a napkin.

An empty milk carton sailed across the room, and the supervisor turned to see if she could discover who'd thrown it.

Corky quickly wiped his finger on Iris's shoulder and ran away. He stopped in the doorway and sang, "It's a sha-a-a-ame! Doot-dee-doodle-de-doot-de-do!" and did some dorky dance moves. Then he walked out, laughing.

Too bad Corky Newton got mustard on Iris's shirt. Her dad had bought it for her at a fund-raiser for the Temporary Contemporary Art Museum in L.A. It had a skeleton dressed like a cowboy on the front, sitting in a saloon playing poker. On the back was an open hand of cards. It was even signed by the guy who made it—Bill Wiley, number 186 of a limited edition of two hundred.

Iris pulled her sleeve around; there was mustard on the shoulder and mustard on the queen of spades. Too bad Corky Newton had decided to ruin it. Too bad—for him.

Iris looked over at the lunch supervisor, who was interrogating some boys. "Now, which one of y'all threw that drank?" she asked them.

They pointed to their chests and shook their heads no.

Iris strolled across the room, casually stopping to help herself to an enormous yellow jug of mustard that was sitting on the snack bar near a sign that said DO NOT REMOVE!

She carried it outside and gazed across the courtyard. She hid the mustard container between the leaves of a potted palm, shoved back toward the trunk. Corky had vanished—but never mind.

She'd have other opportunities.

Iris sat down on the steps. She stretched out her legs and crossed them at the ankles. She wasn't so sure about her rattlesnake high-tops; nobody had even noticed them. She needed Nike Airs. Or Reebok Pumps. When were the tryouts for the basketball team?

She looked at her chest, then down again at her shoes.

She needed Nike Airs or Reebok Pumps, and she also needed a white sweatshirt like Stella had and she needed to fill it out like Stella did and she needed to know whether or not she was going to have a flat chest for the rest of her life like Mrs. Fuller's sister Irene.

Iris watched the music teacher cross the yard, wearing bright-green pants and carrying a black case that contained a large musical instrument—probably a tuba. Tomorrow in homeroom she would put a suggestion in the student council suggestion box that there should be a dress code for teachers: Faculty members wearing kelly-green pants should be thrown into jail. What was taking Jennifer and Stella so long to finish eating, anyway?

Iris needed to make more friends. But she didn't exactly know how. And even if she did, she didn't have the time. All of her spare time at school was spent in the library, as she frantically tried to finish what she was supposed to have done the day before. Half the time, she didn't know whether she was coming or going. She'd already lost her math notebook and a denim jacket that cost eighty dollars. What she needed was a locker organizer like Jennifer's, because being organized was by far the hardest thing about junior high—besides figuring out how to dress down for PE without letting anybody see your bra.

She stood up.

What time was it?

A little round paper reinforcement was stuck to her knee. She quickly peeled it off. A hair was stuck to it. She glanced around to see if anybody was looking. Then she rolled it up between her fingers and flicked it into the bushes. She looked down at her knees.

Were people supposed to shave their knees?

Iris didn't know. Of course, Mrs. Edna Beanbrain Fuller would have been more than happy to discuss the topic with Iris, along with every other personal aspect of Iris's physical and emotional development—if Iris had any interest in talking to her about knee hairs or anything else, which she didn't.

She wanted to talk to her mother.

The warning bell rang. Iris kicked a pebble the whole way across the asphalt. She walked slowly to her locker. The cheerleaders were standing around it, chatting with Cindi.

"Hieee!" said Cindi to Iris.

"Hi," said Iris.

Cindi made a stupid face and looked at the ceiling. "Uhma gahd!"

"What!" said one of her friends.

"Dist wait one second, 'kay?" said Cindi.

Then she rested her hand on Iris's shoulder and said, in baby talk: "Sorry! I need to get back into my locker. I forgot I need my pom-poms!" Suddenly, her eyes grew very round. "Uhma gahd! Turn around! What happened to your shurt?"

"Corky Newton," said Iris.

"E-e-e-e-w!" cried Cindi. "He, like, totally . . . Look at it!"

"I know," said Iris.

"Bum-mer," said Cindi.

"Bum-mer," said the other girls.

"Is he that dweeb with the bomber jacket?" asked one of the cheerleaders.

"Yup," said somebody.

"I heard he was the one that threw gum in Morgan's hair during the pep rally," said Cindi. She glanced up at her friends. "You know that perm she had to have cut off? It cost, like, *seventy dollars!*"

Cindi found her pom-poms and closed her locker. She looked again at Iris's shirt and made a very, *very* sad face. "And it was such a cute shurt, like, rully cute. . . ."

"I know," said Iris. "I really loved this shirt— my dad got it for me in L.A."

"Bum-mer," said Cindi again. She poked out her bottom lip and looked sadly at the other cheerleaders. They made sad faces.

Then they got happy again and left.

Iris opened her locker and rummaged through it.

Cindi had hung an air freshener inside her

locker. The fumes leaked into Iris's locker and made everything smell like bathroom deodorizer.

Why wasn't her math book in her locker?

Iris slammed the door closed before she got asphyxiated. Deciding she needed a drink of water before class started, she hurried down the hall to the fountain. The hall was crowded. When she leaned over to get a drink, somebody splashed water into her face.

She whirled around, but she didn't see who'd done it. There was just a sea of students, walking away in both directions. She went into the bathroom, where three or four popular girls were making quick adjustments to their makeup. Nobody spoke. Iris dried her face with a paper towel. She looked up into the mirror, and as soon as the girls left, she got an eye goober out of the corner of her eye. There was an eyelash floating around on her eyeball.

The bell rang before she got it out.

She hurried to math.

Mr. Farny stopped talking as Iris sat down. "I was just saying," he said to Iris, "that there will be a homework quiz on Monday—"

Corky Newton spoke from the back of the room. "Aren't you supposed to get a pass from the office when you're late?"

"So," continued Mr. Farny, "everybody needs to check the list of assignments posted on the back wall." He opened the coat closet and hung his tweed jacket on a hanger.

"Hey!" whispered Corky. "Iris!"

She turned and stared at him.

"You're supposed to *drank* from a water fountain, darlin'," he whispered, in his best imitation of the noon supervisor. "Drank! Not warsh your face in it!"

He frowned at the boy beside him. "And lowrd! Would you look at that *shirt!*" he said, resting his hand on his chest. "In' it a *may-ess?*"

"Newton?" said Mr. Farny.

He waited until Corky looked up at him.

"Shut your trap."

SEVEN

$\mathcal{I}$ris parted the curtains and looked at the new neighbors' house.

It was a beautiful two-story shingled house, covered with ivy. Next to the garage was a potting shed, and beside the shed was an empty aviary.

Maybe birds would nest in it soon.

Mrs. Fuller stood on her tiptoes behind Iris to see out the window. "See anybody?"

Iris jerked the curtain closed.

"Well, they've moved in," said Mrs. Fuller. "And that boy we saw yesterday at the underpants shop? He's the new neighbors' kid; I knew I'd seen him someplace. I spoke to him this morning."

Iris turned around. "You . . . spoke to him?"

"Yes. I asked him why he wasn't in school. He's not going to start till next week. And in the eighth grade—can you imagine it?"

Yes, Iris could imagine it. And she could imagine other things, like how nice it was going to be when Mrs. Fuller pinned her little pillbox hat into her blue perm and picked up her pink Samsonite suitcase and headed on down the road.

Mrs. Fuller brushed off the front of her skirt and tugged on it to adjust the fit. "In the eighth grade and skipping school! I told him, though: I told him it's truancy not to go to school."

She put her hands on her hips.

"And to tell his parents I said so."

Iris groaned. "Oh, great." She frowned at Mrs. Fuller for a minute. "By the way," she asked her, "what time are you leaving tomorrow?"

"I don't know," said Mrs. Fuller. "But there's yellow paint on the back of your shirt. You should be more careful when you paint—"

"It's mustard," said Iris. "Okay? Somebody walked into me holding a bagel dog."

"Why were you walking and eating?"

"I wasn't walking and eating!"

"Well, you should look out when other people are eating," said Mrs. Fuller, "and walking. Mustard stains! Anyway, let's see. . . . I should wait to take in the mail, I suppose. And do the watering." She frowned and began making a clicking noise with her tongue. "And air your parents' bedding . . ."

She wrinkled her nose.

"About ten-thirty," she said. "If the mail comes on time. And I'll be at Irene's by two."

Iris smiled. Good. By ten-thirty, the Martian would be out of the house. It would be a little strange, coming home to an empty house—but she could handle it. Maybe she'd invite Maggie over to spend the night. They could take a pizza out of the freezer for dinner; they could stay up late watching TV. They could call a couple of boys and say it was Jennifer. They could call Corky Newton and say he'd won something—like a lifetime supply of fish ice cream.

Good old Mag! Iris went into the hallway to use the phone. She dialed Maggie's number, and Maggie answered. "Hi," said Iris.

"Hi," said Maggie.

"Did I tell you about going to the mall and getting the rattlesnake high-tops with Mrs. Fuller?"

"Yup."

"But now I'm not sure I like them. They make my feet look big."

"Your feet are big."

"Anyway, there were glow-in-the-dark fluorescent-orange skeleton socks there on sale, from Halloween. But Mrs. Fuller said no. Can you believe it?"

"You told me. . . . Mom says I have to do my homework," said Maggie.

"Well, call me when you're done," said Iris, "so I can tell you about the puppet I'm making that attacks and totally *wastes* Corky Newthead's two-hundred-dollar hand-painted European puppet. Unless I already told you."

Iris hung up the phone and began counting slowly. There was nobody on earth who hated Corky Newton more than Maggie Hunter. Last year, he'd even gotten her suspended from school.

When she got to four, the phone rang. She picked it up. "Out of the wolf-heads!" cried Iris. "From Bernadette's!"

"Yes!" cried Maggie. "Yes! I love it!"

"Of course, I'll have to make certain . . . modifications," Iris told her.

"Of course," said Maggie.

"For some surprise special effects . . ."

"What special effects?" said Maggie.

"Guts!" cried Iris. "Guts! And blood! And gore!" She heard Maggie's mother talking in the background.

"I love it!" said Maggie. "Okay, I'm coming!" she called to her mother.

"I *have* to do my homework," said Maggie.

"And I got my pictures back," said Iris. "And oh! One other thing. That family that moved in next door to me? They have a kid."

"Boy or girl?"

"Boy," said Iris.

"How old?" said Maggie.

"Don't know," said Iris. "Maybe fourteen."

"Cute?"

"Totally. Anyway, can you come over after school tomorrow?"

"Tomorrow? Till what time?"

"To spend the night," said Iris.

"Call you back," said Maggie. She hung up the phone.

Iris went into her room and lay on her bed on top of some books and papers. The bedspread was wadded up. She wasn't comfortable.

She kicked and shoved whatever would move onto the rug and lay with her head on her pillow and stared up underneath her canopy. What was that on top of her canopy? She stood up and punched the eyelet material, and a piece of dried-out pizza, maybe a month old, flew into the air and onto the floor.

She lay back down.

Maybe she should have mentioned to Maggie that Mrs. Martian would be gone—that they would be alone. But maybe Maggie's mother wouldn't approve, and if she found out, Maggie would be in trouble.

When you thought about it, really, why should Maggie's mother care? She couldn't stand Mrs. Fuller, either. Anybody could see that. Anyway, Iris and Maggie would be home playing, just like any other time—they didn't need Mrs. Fuller around to poke her nose into everything.

She waited for the phone to ring.

And Iris would be in charge. Plenty of girls in the seventh grade baby-sat—Iris could easily have been hired to baby-sit a girl in the sixth grade, like Maggie. In fact, maybe she'd ask Maggie to pay her—say, a buck an hour.

Iris smiled to herself. But what if Maggie freaked out that Iris had dumped Mrs. Fuller? What if she told her mother?

The phone rang.

"Tomorrow's Friday," said Maggie. "I forgot. I go to Dad's house."

"Can't you skip it?"

"Skip it?" said Maggie. "No. We don't see each other all week long. And this weekend it's his birthday."

"Oh," said Iris.

"But I could come over for a while after school,

maybe," said Maggie. "And he could pick me up there."

"Your dad?" said Iris. She thought a minute. Maggie's father was a lawyer. He would be the first person to figure out that Iris had ditched Mrs. Fuller.

"No. That's okay." She paused for an awkward moment. "I thought you said you have to do your homework."

"I know," said Maggie. "Bye!"

"Bye," said Iris. She hung up the phone. Was it against the law for a kid to spend the night alone? Iris's stomach fluttered. Why would it be against the law? Oh, anyway. Tomorrow would be fun—it would go by fast. She could go to the mall after school . . . and get the wolf-head underpants at Bernadette's. The idea was too great to give up on.

Iris looked down at her shirt. She could see herself in the mirror on her closet door. She sat taller, with her shoulders straight.

The truth was, she didn't have much to show for her twelve and a half years. The only things that had grown lately were her feet.

In fact, looking down on them, her rattlesnake high-tops did look a little like gunboats. Did Mrs. Fuller have any information about when feet quit growing?

Last year, the other kids looked up to Iris. She had been an early bloomer; she towered over most of the boys. She could stand eyeball to eyeball with any kid in the school.

But junior high was different. Nobody knew that nobody messes with Iris Bloom. Nobody even knew who she was! She'd lost her standing; she'd lost her stature! Some of the girls from the other feeder schools were as big as her mother; some bleached their hair. Some looked like teachers, from behind.

Stella, Jennifer—even Hilary—had filled out admirably over the summer. And Hilary had gotten contact lenses and a perm.

Iris went to the mirror and began brushing her hair. Should she get a perm? Should she ask her mother if she could henna her hair? Iris turned around and checked out how she looked from the rear. Weren't her hips a little large, in relation to the rest of her?

She pushed her bedroom door closed, to avoid having to listen to Mrs. Fuller talking to herself about how much stuff she had to fit into one small suitcase. She had listened to Mrs. Fuller long enough already; at dinner she had yakked through two generous helpings of macaroni and cheese, then through Jell-O mold with pineapple in it. Iris wasn't interested—in macaroni and

85

cheese, in Jell-O mold, or in anything Mrs. Fuller had to say.

She glanced at the clock; she couldn't think of anything else to do to put off doing her homework. Except maybe she should look in on Ivy Lou. She peered into the plastic box. "Good evening, grumpbucket!" said Iris.

Ivy Lou retreated as far into her shell as she could.

Iris picked her up. She could see three of her little hairy pointed legs and her fat claw. "See that purple shell?" said Iris. "I paid two-fifty for it." She frowned and set Ivy Lou back onto the gravel and put the purple shell beside her.

"Put it on!" Iris whispered, gruffly.

She wandered around her room. Where was her pack? She needed a Guess bag like Lydia had, instead of a pack. She hated her stupid pack.

She looked out her bedroom window into the neighbors' driveway. A beautiful tomcat was sitting under the garage light, licking its paw and cleaning its whiskers.

Would the boy be walking to school? Or would they drive him in the BMW? She picked up her brush from the windowsill. Had he or had he not seen her looking at the padded bra?

She discovered her pack hiding behind the wastebasket and sat down in the corner of her bedroom, on the lap of the stuffed gorilla. Its chin rested on top of her head. She found her notebook that had pictures of lips and elephants and a sticker that said SAVE THE ELEPHANTS—DON'T BUY IVORY on the front.

She flipped through it until she found the "Boy Who Cried Wolf" script.

"The Boy Who Cried Wolf," she read. "Fable by Aesop—Script by Iris Bloom."

She had already written four and a half pages in the library at school. And she'd done an excellent job on the dialogue, if she did say so herself. And now she was at the good part—the part where the boy was out playing for the last time. She had stopped just after he saw something gray and hairy moving through the trees.

Iris chewed on the end of her pencil.

"BOY looks puzzled," she wrote.

She thought a minute, then continued writing:

BOY
What's that large and hairy gray thing
moving through the trees?

87

*[Nobody answers him. Because every-
body is in the house. BOY stupidly ap-
proaches trees to get a better look.
Suddenly, he lets out a BLOODCUR-
DLING SCREAM.]*

BOY
[screaming]
Help! Oh, my God—help me! It's a
wolf!

*[He puts his hands on his chest and
screams again. Then he puts his hands
in the air and screams again and
again. At this moment, a loud, snarl-
ing noise is heard, and out leaps the
WOLF.]*

WOLF
Aha! You little dweeb! Isn't it a little
dumb to walk up to something large
and hairy standing behind a tree?

BOY
Help! A wolf!

WOLF

Oh, "Help! A wolf!" Give me a break!
Do you think anybody would listen to
you, you lying little wimp? Everybody
knows you're a liar, you creep!

*[WOLF loudly laughs, then pounces
upon the BOY, grabbing his arm in her
jaws. BOY screams in pain, again and
again.]*

WOLF

Now I've got you, and what a tasty
morsel you shall be. You stink; and
you've got a big fat gut and a big fat
butt, and all the tastier you will be for
a wolf.

BOY

Somebody help me! There's a wolf out
here! And she's sinking her teeth into
my arm!

*[At this moment, a package of some-
thing red that stains bursts open inside the WOLF's mouth, splattering red*

stuff that looks like blood every-where.]

BOY

My God! Help me! The wolf—she's tearing off my arm!

[WOLF tears off the BOY's arm and spits it out. Then, with a frightening howl, she springs into the air, and taking the BOY's head into her enor-mous jaws—]

"Thirsty?" said Mrs. Fuller.

Iris looked up and growled.

"I made us some hot chocolate," said Mrs. Fuller.

Mrs. Fuller was standing in the doorway, wearing an orange terry cloth robe, bright-green socks, and bright-green slippers. Iris couldn't help thinking: *Too bad Halloween is over.* Mrs. Fuller could have stood on her head and looked like a pumpkin.

Iris closed her notebook and sighed.

Mrs. Fuller shuffled over and handed her a mug of hot chocolate. She pointed to the cover of the notebook with her foot. "Why not buy Ivory? They make soap out of elephants?"

Iris didn't answer.

"Soon I see Irene," said Mrs. Fuller, blowing into her mug of chocolate and slurping it.

Iris blew on her chocolate. "Yup."

"It should be fun," said Mrs. Fuller.

Iris felt an unexpected little wave of fear. Would it really be okay for her to come home from school to an empty house? To stay the night alone?

Mrs. Fuller belched loudly. "It's the macaroni and cheese," she said. She slurped and burped again. "Or the pineapple."

Yes.

Iris was sure she could manage it.

EIGHT

*I*ris woke up to the sound of the vacuum. Why would anybody be vacuuming at seven o'clock in the morning?

She lay there a minute, listening to the noise grow louder and louder as Mrs. Fuller headed down the hall. Would it be too late to tell Mrs. Fuller that her parents weren't coming home till tomorrow?

Iris got out of bed. She pulled off her nightgown and threw it on the floor. She stood there, naked and yawning.

Suddenly, the door flew open and Mrs. Fuller charged in. "Morning, glory!" she shouted.

Iris grabbed her nightgown and held it in front of her and quickly backed up against the wall. She watched as Mrs. Fuller cleaned her rug, flipping the vacuum cleaner cord behind her with one hand.

"Get dressed!" shouted Mrs. Fuller.

Get dressed? Was she crazy? Iris backed farther away.

Mrs. Fuller stomped on the black plastic on-off button. "What do you think you're hiding?" she said, with a grin. "I can see your bee-hind in the mirror!"

Iris let go of her nightgown with one hand and tried to cover her rear with the other, but the nightgown fell partway down—exposing her front, which she frantically tried to shield with her arm.

Mrs. Fuller wasn't looking.

She was laughing—laughing like a hyena—and dragging the vacuum cleaner out of the room by the hose.

Iris stormed over and slammed the door and locked it. Then she threw her nightgown on her bed and climbed into her underpants. She put her bra around her waist to do the little hook, then turned it around and pulled it up and got her arms into it. Rats! It was twisted.

So she had to start all over again.

Soon she was dressed—in cut-offs and a Michael Jordan T-shirt that had BULLS printed on the front.

She sat down on the rug. Where on earth were some socks?

She looked under her bed. Why wouldn't Mrs. Fuller let her get the skeleton socks? She was the one who had said Iris needed socks. So what if Halloween was past!

Iris stood up and stormed over to her sock drawer and yanked it open. Inside was dust and two socks: one bumblebee striped and one black and white checked. Oh, well. At least they were the right thickness!

She pulled them on, then put on her high-tops and laced them up. Then she checked out her outfit in the mirror. Did she look great!

She bent over and brushed her hair upside down, as hard as she could, and pulled it into a ponytail. She wrapped a terry cloth ponytail holder around it. And fluffed up her bangs. And squirted them with Superspritz.

"You," she said aloud, "are going to have a wonderful, *wonderful* time without Mrs. Bean-brain." Blowing herself a kiss in the mirror, she went down the hall into the bathroom, splashed some water on her face, dried herself on a towel, and stuffed the towel behind the towel rack.

She went into the kitchen. "We're out of milk," announced Mrs. Fuller. "Tell your mother."

"No chocolate milk?"

"I used it for the hot chocolate."

Iris made herself a bowl of Frosted Flakes with orange juice. It wasn't bad. But it wasn't good.

Mrs. Fuller started giggling.

"What's funny?" said Iris.

"Oh, nothing," said Mrs. Fuller. ". . . and standing right in front of a *mirror*," she mumbled to herself. She giggled again, then took her flowered hankie out of her robe pocket and wiped her eyes with it.

Was that the same hankie she'd been sticking in her nose?

Iris looked down at her cereal bowl.

"Tell me the plan," said Mrs. Fuller. "What's the plan?"

Iris put a huge spoonful of cereal in her mouth and said, "If Mom and Dad are late, I call the FBI."

"No!" said Mrs. Fuller. "Call the Blackmans. They'll be home till six. The number is in the drawer. Right on top. So what do you do?"

Iris chewed and swallowed. "I give up," she said. "What?"

"You call the Blackmans!" repeated Mrs. Fuller. She sighed and drummed her fingers on her chest. "I've left a note too, right *here* beside the cookbooks, for your parents." She slapped the note that was on the counter. "Have you got your keys?"

"No," said Iris.

"Yes, you do," said Mrs. Fuller. "I pinned them

inside your schoolbag when you were asleep. So if your mother and father are not *home* when you get here, turn *off* the alarm with the alarm key and *unlock* the door with the door key and *call* Mrs. Blackman. She'll be right over; I called her last night to remind her."

Iris sighed. What time was it, anyway? She finished her cereal and swallowed the little vitamin pill beside her bowl. "Well, bye," she said.

Mrs. Fuller followed Iris into her room, carrying her lunch. "Have fun with Irene," said Iris.

"Here," said Mrs. Fuller. She put Iris's lunch in her pack and jingled the two keys that were pinned inside. "See?"

Iris nodded. "Thanks."

"Well, you've been a good girl," said Mrs. Fuller. "A real good girl—I told your mother in the note."

"Thanks," said Iris. She picked up her pack and looked at Mrs. Fuller.

Mrs. Fuller put her arms around Iris and squeezed her cheek against Iris's cheek. "You know," she said to Iris, "I never had a daughter of my own—or a son. So of course, now I don't have any grandchildren. . . ."

She peered through her eyeglasses into Iris's eyes. "Oh, I know I'm just an old bat—Irene's the same. We never had much luck when it came to family. Course we have each other. . . .

"But you're about the closest I've ever had to having a little girl. I've had a good time here, standing in the place of your mother, and it's been an honor, taking over—like a family member would—what with your parents so far away."

Mrs. Fuller's eyes looked a little misty.

"And oh, I know I'm not much of a mother or a grandmother, but I just wanted to let you know that I think—well, what I told you! You're just a real good girl," she said quietly, and stood looking at Iris and blinking.

For some reason, Iris felt really rotten.

For about a minute.

She hugged Mrs. Fuller good-bye and went outside and headed down the path. Leaves scratched across the sidewalk. She said Ha! in the air to test the temperature. It was pretty cold.

She glanced at the house next door.

She hoped the boy in the house next door wasn't looking out the window. Saying Ha! to test the temperature was a fairly nerdy thing to do.

She hurried down Locust Street. Ahead of her, she saw Hilary get out of her mother's station wagon and wave good-bye. Iris caught up with her at the entrance to the school.

"I have the perfect, *perfect* idea for the wolf puppet," Iris told her. She took Hilary aside by the stairwell and told her about the wolf-head underpants at Bernadette's and her plan for the puppet and the special effects.

Hilary approved and said she wouldn't tell anybody. When Jennifer showed up, Iris ran through the idea again. Hilary got nervous and left, but not before suggesting that Iris should consider barbecue sauce as a possibility for the special effects. She and her family had gone to McDonald's the night before, and her mother had accidentally rested her elbow in a package of the sauce that came with the Chicken McNuggets— quite a disaster. Her cashmere sweater would have to be specially cleaned. It might even be ruined forever.

Jennifer and Iris hurried to their lockers, whispering and laughing. And ran into Cindi, who, along with a couple of the other cheerleaders, thought the idea was, like, totally awesome.

Rully!

After homeroom, a few of them met again just outside the girls' bathroom. This time, Jennifer had brought Stella along—to let her in on the secret. They went into the bathroom and passed around a tube of pink lip gloss—and rambled on and on to one another in the mirror.

"Late!" shouted Corky Newton as the girls walked happily through the door.

Mrs. Gersen ignored him. She looked around the room. "Lenore is absent again?" She made a little mark in her book.

"She's probably pretending to be sick so she doesn't have to take the test on figures of speech," Corky announced loudly. "She's probably playing hooky."

Figures of speech! What were figures of speech? Iris had completely forgotten to study!

"Mrs. Gersen?" said Corky.

"Hold on a minute, will you?" said Mrs. Gersen. She stared down the rows of desks. "Christine Bednark. Absent." She frowned. "Where *is* everybody?"

"Faking," said Corky. "Just like Lenore Allen. They're trying to get out of the test. Mrs. Gersen?"

"Quiet," said Mrs. Gersen. "Okay, Corky? Please!"

Mrs. Gersen finished looking at some papers on the top of her desk.

Corky Newton began waving his hand frantically. "Could William and me do 'The Boy Who Cried Wolf' instead of letting Iris be the wolf?" he said. "Could we? Please?"

Mrs. Gersen looked at him. "William and I," said Mrs. Gersen.

"Could William be the wolf? He hasn't made

99

his stag puppet yet; he could make a wolf instead. Couldn't you, William?"

William nodded yes.

"I'll help him," said Corky.

"No," said Mrs. Gersen.

"Please!" cried Corky. "And Iris could be the stag. She was acting like the world's expert on antlers yesterday—why doesn't *she* make the stag!"

"Yeah!" said William, in a deep voice. "I want to be the wolf; let Iris be the stag. I hate stags! And besides, I don't know how to make a mane out of tinfoil."

Mrs. Gersen closed her eyes for a moment. "A *mane* out of *tinfoil?*" she whispered. "On a deer?" She opened her eyes again.

"Iris?" she said.

Iris looked up.

"It's up to you," said Mrs. Gersen. "Would you like to have William be the wolf in 'The Boy Who Cried Wolf' and you be the stag? You had some excellent ideas about the stag puppet. . . ."

"No, thank you," said Iris.

Corky Newton sighed.

"I don't want to make the stag puppet," said Iris. "I want to make the wolf puppet. Yesterday afternoon, I developed a . . . design for the wolf puppet."

"Developed a design," muttered Corky Newton. "*Give* me a break."

"And anyway," continued Iris, "I certainly wouldn't want to give up the rare opportunity of appearing in a performance with a two-hundred-dollar hand-carved European dweeb in lederhosen."

"That's quite enough," said Mrs. Gersen.

"Sorry," said Iris. She chuckled behind her hand and then leaned over and whispered something about the satin wolf-head underpants to Nadia, who laughed.

"Please take out your textbooks," said Mrs. Gersen, "and turn to the section on adverbial phrases—page thirty-six."

Iris glanced over her shoulder at Corky, who had narrowed his eyelids to slits and was sticking out his chin in her direction. They stared at each other until Mrs. Gersen said, "Textbooks!" in a sharp voice.

Corky opened his desktop. Iris turned around and leafed through her book.

Nadia raised her hand. "May I please sharpen my pencil?" she asked.

"Yes," said Mrs. Gersen.

When Nadia stood up, she slipped Iris a note.

"Your kiding," the note said. "Mens underpants made of wulf? You MUST be kiding!!!!!!!!"

"Not made of wolf—made in the shape of a wolf's head," whispered Iris, when Nadia passed back by.

"Girls?" said Mrs. Gersen. She pressed her finger against her lips and frowned.

Nadia sat down.

"Lydia?" said Mrs. Gersen. "Would you go to the office and get me some staples? For a standard stapler. Thanks."

Lydia stood up and smiled. She was impeccably dressed in white tennis shoes and socks, a white sweatshirt, and pale-pink Guess jeans.

Iris found a pencil in her pack; it was chewed up. The eraser was gone. And the metal eraser sheath was chewed closed. How come she never had any nice pencils with purple stars and tassels, like Lydia? Because she wasn't Lydia. So she didn't have spiral binders full of new paper, either—or a canvas Guess bag to carry them around in.

Iris looked through her notebook for a clean sheet of paper, but there wasn't any. There were pages and pages with "Iris Bloom Iris Bloom Iris Bloom" written across them in cursive. Iris was looking for a new way to sign her name.

She finally found a sheet of paper with only one small doodle on it. She turned it over and wrote: "Design for the Wolf Puppet to Be Made from Underpants."

She drew a picture of a wolf's head with an ugly expression and its tongue hanging out. Then she added a person's legs and feet underneath it. And hairs on the legs.

Above the head, she drew a big gut and a belly button, a chest, arms, a neck, and a face with cross-eyes and fangs.

Below it, she wrote: "Corky."

She folded the paper in half. And slyly handed it to Stella, who giggled.

"Girls?" said Mrs. Gersen. She pressed her finger on her lips and frowned again.

Stella and Iris looked down at their books.

Lydia returned from the office with a box of staples. Stella poked the note into her sweatshirt pocket as she passed by. "Give it to Ceclie," whispered Stella.

But Lydia ignored her.

She sat down at her desk and opened the paper and stared at the drawing. "I'm telling!" she whispered.

"Shut up!" whispered Stella. "Pass it to Ceclie."

Lydia quickly passed the note to Ceclie, who opened it and snorted out loud in an attempt to keep from laughing.

Mrs. Gersen looked up from her lesson plan book, straight into Iris's eyes. "I mean it," she said, sternly. "You girls are going to end up getting detention. You think I'm kidding?"

No. They didn't think she was kidding. Still, the note made its way around to practically every girl in the room without anybody getting detention.

And practically every girl in the room ended up sitting with Iris at lunch—even Lydia—chatting and giggling about what a good idea it was for Iris to make a puppet out of a wolf-head G-string and reminding one another that Mrs. Gersen had suggested that people be inventive and creative and so on, and how great it would look in the case outside the office.

And they all sat together at the pep rally, too, joined by a few other girls—in particular, a couple of very, *very* popular eighth-grade girls on the student council, who admired the drawing and approved of the idea and congratulated Iris on her plan.

Word had really gotten around. After the rally was over, Cindi announced that there was a special cheer—she'd made it up and choreographed it. The cheerleaders changed their formation.

"Look out! Look out!" they yelled together. "Va-va-voom!"

They began getting up on each other's backs.

"Here comes Iris. Iris Bloom!"

Morgan, with her perm cut off and her new step haircut, ended up on top of the pyramid, looking a little like Woody Woodpecker.

"Iris—Iris," they hollered, "give her room. Go, go get 'em, Iris Bloom!"

Then they all yelled: "L-o-o-o-o-o-o-k *out!*" and jumped down and shook their pom-poms in Iris's direction and ran away.

By the end of the day, Iris had practically reached celebrity status. Kids who hardly even knew her were coming up and patting her on the back and saying things like: "Just do it!"—even a few cute boys. By the time school was over and she had waved good-bye and the kids on the bus had hooted and hollered and given her thumbs-up, Iris was stoked.

How mad would her parents get if they found out she'd ditched Mrs. Fuller?

Iris couldn't have cared less.

She set her course and headed down Locust Street with a full head of steam.

NINE

*I*ris glanced down the driveway before she climbed the porch steps. "Good," she whispered. Mrs. Fuller's car was gone.

Looking in her pack, she found and unpinned her keys. Then she turned off the alarm system with one key and opened the door with the other.

"Mrs. Fuller?" she called. Nobody answered; she shut the door behind her. The house was dark and quiet.

Iris put the keys on the hat stand and undid her ponytail holder and shook her hair loose. Her head hurt; she rubbed her scalp.

Sometimes it was painful to be cool.

She walked into the kitchen. The mail was on the table, along with a note written to her parents. "Dear Mr. and Mrs. Bloom," it said. "Welcome home. What's left of the money is on top of the refrigerator; I bought new sneaks for Iris yesterday. . . ."

Sneaks?

"They cost $28.00. Her film development was twenty-three bucks, but that's art for you. Things went well. I watered this morning. I threw out all the newspapers, except Sunday's TV magazine. I've gone to my sister Irene's in Vallejo—will be there through Sunday. That darn crab in there pinches and cost a fortune. It was Mrs. Hunter that okayed it, not me. Sincerely, Edna Fuller."

Iris read through the note again. She looked at the top of the note. Was it dated? No. She searched through a basket on the counter and found a pen with blue ink in it, then shook it and scribbled some loops on the cover of the phone book, to make sure the ink was running.

"P.S.," she wrote on the bottom of the note, in her best imitation of Mrs. Fuller's handwriting. "I had to leave just a little before you got here—to get to Irene's in time for an appointment. I've asked the neighbors if it's okay for Iris to sit on their porch for just those few minutes till you get here, and they said they'd keep an eye on her."

Iris chewed on the pen for a minute. "But she really doesn't need to be looked after every second of the day," she added. "She's very machure." Iris examined her handiwork. Not bad.

She pulled a chair over to the refrigerator. She found two twenties on top—way more than she expected to find. Mrs. Fuller, that rat, had said she was out of money when she said no to those great fuzzy socks with orange fluorescent skeletons printed on them.

Well, she could get them this afternoon.

Iris jumped down off the chair and stuffed the money in the pocket on the front of her T-shirt. She wondered: How close could you get to lying without actually lying?

She looked in on Ivy Lou, who was asleep inside her shell. Ivy Lou had become more and more lazy every day. What was the problem?

Iris pulled her shirt over her head and dropped it on the rug. Then she opened her closet door, yanked a B.U.M. Equipment sweatshirt off the shelf, and pulled it on. She got the money out of her T-shirt pocket, then rummaged through her dresser for more. She found change and the tube of her mother's lipstick, which she carefully put on.

Iris looked at the clock; it was three twenty-five. She stood there for a minute, thinking—and listening to the clock tick. There was lots of time to walk downtown; it was only a mile or so, and it couldn't take more than half an hour.

And her new sneakers were comfortable; she jumped up and down on them a few times and pulled up the tops of her socks.

She grabbed her keys off the hat stand, turned on the burglar alarm, and walked outside, closing the door behind her. She checked the handle; the door was locked.

What a great afternoon! A breeze was lifting the branches of the pines as Iris headed down the path to the sidewalk. She turned to look at her house. She'd set the alarm; the stove wasn't on; the door was locked. Everything was okay.

She hoped.

Iris took a deep breath. The air was exhilarating. Boy, this was going to be something—going to the mall by herself.

Where was the mall, anyway?

She'd been there a thousand times; she'd know where to turn. She'd know how to get there. And she'd do fine, once she got there. There were millions of kids at the mall by themselves; all the junior high kids hung out there, in groups of twos and threes. And Iris was in junior high; only one and a half years, and she'd be in high school.

Only a few more years, and she'd be driving a car!

There was a large park on the corner of Locust and Highgate. Iris cut through the trees on a utility road, stopping for a drink at a water fountain made of stones. An elderly couple were standing in the gazebo, holding hands.

A gardener was trimming some bushes with large metal shears near a shed where somebody had written "Marguerite and The Dood" in spray paint. And sprayed a big pink heart.

Iris hurried across the grass on a stone path decorated with chips of Spanish tile and pushed through some bushes onto Highgate Avenue, where a few people were waiting for a bus. Should she take the bus?

No. She didn't know which bus to take to the mall. But she knew how to walk there, so she continued on—crossing at crosswalks after waiting for the little green man to light up, and checking both ways to make sure some drunk wasn't running the light.

Within ten or fifteen minutes, she could see the huge brick complex; she could see the Macy's sign on the tallest building. See? It didn't take long. She put her hand in her pocket and jingled the change. Then she stopped and pulled out the bills; it was all there: two twenties and three ones. Good. She stuffed it back into her pocket and, softly singing a Madonna song, headed toward the mall—stepping twice in every square of the sidewalk to avoid the cracks.

Soon Iris was walking through the huge brick entrance to the mall. She stopped to admire a granite rock wrapped in bronze—some kind of sculpture. Two boys came over and sat near her on a green chain fence—two children who couldn't have been in more than the fourth or fifth grade.

She put her nose in the air and walked inside.

The artificial lighting made things look weird; the people looked weird too, hurrying in all directions. Iris saw a pack of pretty girls milling around in front of a Mrs. Fields cookie stand; ordinarily, she would have stopped to buy a chocolate-chip cookie with macadamia nuts—but not this time.

The girls were older than she was and looked as if they might say something about her. In fact, Iris could tell they were saying nasty things about her behind her back when she passed Mrs. Fields, so she whirled around and glared at them for a minute, but they didn't seem to notice.

She shaded her eyes with one hand and squinted beyond them—as if she were trying to see something.

Then she turned and entered Bernadette's.

"You're back!" said the woman.

"For the wolf," said Iris.

The woman went behind the counter and took it off its plexiglass holder. She put it on the counter. "You're *sure* this time?" She looked at Iris without smiling.

What a creep.

"Yes," said Iris. "And the bra . . ."

The woman raised her eyebrows. "For your . . . friend? Thirty-four A?"

"Right."

"Well, you know where they are."

Iris walked over to where the life preservers were hanging. She batted her way through them, until she found a pretty lavender bra with enormous foam cups and a little lacy bow on the front.

"I'd better try it on for her," said Iris.

The woman made a graceful gesture toward the dressing room, and Iris opened the slatted door.

She took off her sweatshirt and put it on the little white bench below the mirror. It was chilly; she got goose bumps. She quickly took off her bra. And looked at the lavender one.

Wow! Was it ever great!

She took it off the tiny plastic hanger and put

it on, then adjusted it and looked in the mirror. She squeezed the cups.

Fantastic! She'd wear it home.

Iris carefully unpinned the paper tags. She put on her sweatshirt; then she put both hands on her stomach and turned sideways. Now, *that* was more like it! "My friend wants me to break it in for her," she said, opening the door. She dropped her old bra into a plastic wastebasket. "So I may as well wear it home."

After an exchange of wolf-head underpants and money, Iris was out the door. She looked at herself in the glass windows of the stores she passed.

Holy Toledo! *What* an improvement!

She stopped and turned sideways and looked over her shoulder at herself in the window of the computer store. Two men walked out. Iris pretended she was fascinated by some color graphics she saw in the display.

She breezed into Marge's store. Going directly to the shell basket, she picked up a knobby green shell for Ivy Lou. "If she doesn't like this one," she loudly announced, "then tough."

Marge came out from behind a rack of cards. "Howdy," she said.

Iris gave her two dollars and waited for change.

"How's the crab?"

"She just sits around," said Iris. "She's a wus."

Marge stared at her.

"I'm serious!" said Iris. "The crab is a wimp!"

"Just wait," said Marge. "She'll come after you. When you least expect it."

Iris left.

She walked into the middle of the mall and surveyed the concession stands. Everything was junk food, Iris's favorite. She settled on potato skins with melted cheese, which she carried in a little checkered paper box to a metal table in the center of the mall. Two nerdy boys walked past her, holding corn dogs; they had plastic walkie-talkies hanging from their belts. Iris closed her eyes and shook her head.

What a couple of dopes!

At the table beside her, a woman sat feeding her little girl bites of soft ice cream with a plastic spoon. The woman opened her own mouth every time the girl opened her mouth, which was covered with melted chocolate ice cream.

Iris missed her mom—even if she couldn't remember a single time her mother ever sat and fed her ice cream. Or gently mopped her chin with a napkin.

And she missed her dad.

Her heart sank a little. She shouldn't have

given Mrs. Fuller the bum's rush; they wouldn't approve of what she did. It was lying, really. And they wouldn't like her hanging out at the mall, alone.

Iris felt terrible.

But oh, come on! She was a woman now, and quite capable of taking care of herself. And, like a woman, Iris sat in the mall eating potato skins with cheese, surveying the scene. Then she had a Coke and a chocolate ice cream. And some onion rings.

Across the way, two teenage girls wearing minishorts and stupid hats were jumping on a trampoline in the lemonade stand, shaking containers of lemonade. They were flushed, but still, they smiled prettily at everyone who passed by.

There wasn't enough money in the world to pay Iris to do a job like that. She peeked into the Bernadette's bag; the wolf-head underpants peeked back at her with little nasty-looking eyes.

Iris opened a corner of a foil package of ketchup. She squeezed it until it burst and splattered onto her onion rings. Perfect! She went back over to the stand and helped herself to several more packages, which she tossed into the bag with the wolf.

Then she sat back down and thought a minute. Maybe she would erase the special effects part from the script. Some things are better left as surprises.

Arthur Frisco might show Mrs. Gersen.

Then again, he might not. Corky had recently begun to refer to him as Captain Anthead.

She ate another onion ring.

She would play it safe. She would erase the special effects part from the script this weekend. And improvise when the time came. By the way, what time was it? A huge lemon-shaped clock was hanging above the lemonade stand.

She jumped up and grabbed her bag. It was almost five-thirty, and she hadn't bought the skeleton socks!

The salesman at Sweet Feet was just turning the sign from OPEN to CLOSED when Iris hurried through the doorway. "The skeleton socks!" she cried, and he smiled warmly.

"Well, I was just on my way out the door, but"—he winked—"for my favorite customer . . . I'll wait." He put his hand on Iris's shoulder, and they walked together across the rug.

"These are the ones," said Iris. She frowned at the size.

"Better try them on," he told her. He tore the sticky paper off the socks and separated them.

Iris sat down and unlaced her sneakers. "Here! Let me help!" he said, kneeling in front of Iris and sliding her foot out of her rattlesnake high-tops. "Are these comfortable?"

"Yup."

He flipped the sneaker into the air and caught it. "Do you think those socks will really glow in the dark?"

"Yup."

He took off her sock. "Nice toenail polish," said the salesman. He pinched her big toe and looked up at Iris.

"Hey!" said Iris, with a giggle.

He picked up a skeleton sock.

"I'll do it," said Iris, taking it from him and putting it on. He watched as she pulled it up high on her calf, then slouched the top down.

She wiggled her toes.

"Good fit," said the salesman, cheerfully, and tickled the bottom of her foot. He stood up and stared at her as she put on the other skeleton sock and laced up her high-tops and double-knotted them.

Iris balled up her old socks and stuck them into the Bernadette's bag. Then she walked up to the counter, digging into her pocket for the money to pay.

The shoe salesman raised both hands in the air and smiled. "Hey!" he told her. "They're on the house!"

Iris stared at him. Then she pulled a five-dollar bill out of her pocket and unwrinkled it.

"No! I mean it!" he said. "These are on the house. They were on sale, anyway—half price. Left over from Halloween." He closed Iris's fingers around the money she was holding and smiled. "Put it away. You're a good customer; it's my way of showing our appreciation."

It was true—Iris was a good customer. She had bought a lot of shoes at Sweet Feet, and so had her mother. And Mrs. Fuller had just spent twenty-eight dollars. Plus tax.

"Besides," he added. "We're neighbors, aren't we?"

Iris frowned. He was a neighbor?

"What street do you live on?" said the shoe salesman.

"Locust," said Iris.

"See? I knew it," he said. He walked with her toward the door. "I thought that's what your mother told me; I live one street over."

"Which street?"

He didn't hear her. He picked up his jacket. "By the way, where is your mother?"

"She's in France," said Iris. "With my dad."

"France! That's a long ways away."

"Well, they'll be home tomorrow," said Iris.

"That's nice," said the man. "I hope they had a wonderful trip." He put on his jacket. They walked together across the rug. "Where's your baby-sitter today?"

Two girls stopped and looked in the doorway.

"Do you have those pink L.A. Gears in size eight?" one called.

"Sorry, ladies," said the man. He held his keys in the air. "I was just closing up."

The girls looked Iris up and down and smirked.

Iris thought they might have been with the group that she had seen earlier—blocking the Mrs. Fields cookie stand. She turned her head away. "Me need a baby-sitter?" she said, in a loud voice. She faked a laugh. "You must be kidding! I'm not down here with a baby-sitter. I'm down here by myself!" Then she whipped her head around and made bug eyes at the girls. "My *parents* are in *Paris*. I *walked* here!"

The girls looked at each other. "What's *her* problem?" one whispered to the other.

"Who *knows*," said the other in a loud voice as they left.

"Well, see you," said Iris to the salesman. She waved as he turned the sign and locked the door.

TEN

*I*ris walked out of the mall. She was surprised to see the street lights glowing pink against the evening sky; she had forgotten that it would be getting dark. A few cars even had their head-lights on.

She pressed the silver WALK button on a pole near the crosswalk and waited for the light to change. After crossing the street, she headed quickly up the sidewalk. In the Dance Gear window, headless plastic mannequins were modeling leotards and tights.

The store was closed. People were hurrying past her. An old woman was wheeling a cart full of groceries down the sidewalk; she had a wart on the end of her nose.

A man wearing mirrored sunglasses stood in the doorway of a bar, smoking a cigarette. Was he looking at Iris? She couldn't tell.

"Hey, Skeleton Socks!" said a voice. Turning, she saw the shoe salesman getting out of his car; he had parked in a yellow zone, leaving the engine running.

"Oh, hi," said Iris.

"Listen," said the salesman, walking over. "Isn't it a little late for you to be walking home alone?"

Iris looked at him.

"Does your mother let you walk home from the mall alone at night?"

"I guess," said Iris.

But Iris knew she wasn't allowed to walk home alone from the mall at night; she wasn't allowed to walk home alone from the mall in the day. And she had just begun to worry a little about it. What if a stranger tried to pick her up?

She'd run away.

What if a stranger in a car slowed down and tried to talk to her?

She wouldn't talk to him; she'd cross the street. She'd yell for help. She'd run away.

"Well, if you don't mind me saying so, you're a little young to be walking home alone in the evening. You're on my way," he said, "and it's getting dark. Why don't you let me give you a ride?"

A ride?

Iris didn't think she really needed a ride.

But on the other hand, it didn't seem like such a great idea to be walking around alone. It was fine past the stores—but the stores were closing. And she would have to walk down Highgate and Locust, where there were hardly any lights. And there were hardly any lights alongside the park.

"Okay," said Iris.

He held the door open; his car was a red Trans Am. She climbed over the gearshift box into the bucket seat.

The salesman got in and closed the door.

Iris looked for her seat belt; she pulled it across her chest and pushed the latch into the holder.

"All set?" said the salesman. He pushed a button, and Iris heard the door locks click. She nodded, and they pulled away from the curb.

Iris looked out the windshield. A plastic square with a silhouette of a bunny on it dangled from the mirror. The car smelled of leather and men's cologne.

"So," said the salesman. "Let's hear some tunes."

Tunes? thought Iris. How embarrassing!

He put a tape into the cassette player, and some dumb soft music began to play. His fingers tapped a rhythm on the steering wheel; Iris looked at the hairs on the back of his hand, at his neat cuffs folded back, at his gold watch.

Then he yawned and stretched his arm and put it over the back of Iris's seat. "So, how old are you, Skeleton Socks?"

"Twelve and a half," said Iris.

She rolled the top of the bag in her lap up tighter and crossed her feet at the ankles.

"Twelve and a half!" said the man. He shook his head. "You must be kidding. I thought you were about sixteen." He looked over at Iris.

He thought she was sixteen? Boy. Maybe the bra did make her look older.

They drove awhile, listening to the music. The salesman drummed his fingers on the uphol-stery on the back of Iris's seat.

"So," he said, "you spent the afternoon at the mall. . . ."

"Right," said Iris. She thought a minute. "You know," she said, "I wasn't really planning to mention to my mother that I went to the mall by myself. I mean, I might, but I might not. She tends to . . . worry about stuff."

The shoe salesman smiled. "Yeah," he said. "I can dig it. My parents used to treat me like a baby, too, when I was growing up."

Iris smiled.

Good. He wouldn't mention it.

"Here we are," she said, pointing to the street

sign at the corner. The man put on his blinker and turned.

"Let me ask you something, Skeleton Socks," said the shoe salesman. He glanced in the rear-view mirror and adjusted it. "What do you think of a guy who likes a girl younger than him?"

Iris looked at the man.

The car rumbled slowly down the street.

"I don't know," she said, because she didn't know. And she didn't know why he would ask her that. "You can speed up," she told him. "My house is up there a ways."

He pulled to the side of the road.

"No," said Iris. "This is the park. My house is farther up."

The man turned off the engine, then turned the key so that the tape would keep playing.

"I'm serious," said the man. "I really want to know: What do you think of a guy who likes a girl younger than him?"

Iris shrugged.

Where was the door handle? She looked near the armrest. "I can just get out here," she said.

"Let me help you," said the salesman. "This gets caught sometimes." He slipped his hand behind the seat belt where it crossed Iris's chest and followed it down to where it met the lap belt.

Iris looked down.

But the man took her chin in his hand and gazed into her eyes. "You know I like you," he told her, in a quiet voice.

Iris's heart thumped. She reached for the seat belt release; but when she tried to push the red button, he covered her hand with his own.

"You know I like you," he whispered again. He picked up her hand and tried to kiss it.

"Don't!" cried Iris, pulling her hand away.

The man laughed softly.

"You know you love it," he whispered. He leaned over and tried to kiss her.

"Stop!" cried Iris. She shoved and elbowed him away. "Leave me alone!"

"And you're a fighter too!" said the man, with an ugly grin. "You naughty thing, you!"

Iris fumbled for the door handle and pulled on it; it was locked. "Unlock the door!" she shouted. "Unlock the door! Let me out!"

She banged on the window with her fist. Then she pulled up on the door handle again and again and kept pushing on the door with her shoulder.

"Take it easy," said the man. "Okay? Just take it easy. I can't unlock the door with you pulling on the handle." He took hold of her arm firmly.

"I'll unlock the door, okay? Just calm down. Hey! I'm sorry."

He let go of her arm.

"Okay?" he said, gently.

"Okay," said Iris. "Just unlock the door so I can get out."

"It's not my fault that I'm attracted to you," said the man, quietly.

It wasn't?

"You're a very attractive lady."

"Can I get out now?" said Iris.

"Sure, you can get out," said the salesman. "But I want to explain something to you first. Okay?"

Iris said nothing.

The man fiddled with the key chain hanging from the ignition. "It's just that I thought you were . . . interested," he said, in a sad way. "I thought you liked me. I thought that's why you let me take you home. But you were just"—he looked over at her—"playing with me."

Playing with him?

"Weren't you!"

Iris didn't answer. What was he talking about?

"Hey, I'm hurt!" said the salesman. "I'm hurt; I'll admit it. But I can deal with rejection!

"I can deal with rejection," he said again,

slumping down in the seat. He folded his arms on his chest and stared blankly at the dashboard. "As long as you don't tell anybody about this. I don't want anybody else getting . . . hurt," he said, and his voice changed to a whisper. He looked sideways at Iris; his eyes frightened her, his voice frightened her.

"Understand what I mean?"

"Yes," said Iris. "There's my friend!" she cried. "Open the door! There's my friend!"

Her new neighbor was trotting down the street after a baseball.

Iris quickly leaned over and blasted the horn; the boy looked toward the car.

"Fine! Get out!" said the shoe salesman. He pushed a button and the door lock clicked open. "But you better keep your mouth shut, you little slut."

Iris quickly pulled on the door handle and got out of the car.

"Wait up!" she called to the boy, who was leaning down looking under a car for the baseball. She ran a few steps. "Wait up!"

The boy looked at her.

Iris waved her Bernadette's bag. "I think we're neighbors," she called. "Aren't we?"

She glanced over her shoulder; the shoe

salesman had started the car. He revved the engine.

"I live in the white house with the green shutters," said Iris. "Right next to your house." She glanced again at the Trans Am. The shoe salesman began a slow turn in the middle of the street.

"Oh, yeah?" said her neighbor. "I lost a baseball in back of that house. That's all I've been doing all afternoon—losing baseballs." With a grunt, he moved farther under the car. "There you are!" he said to the ball, retrieving it from behind the front tire. He stood up and brushed himself off.

"What are those, nuclear socks?" he said.

"Glow-in-the-dark," said Iris. Somehow, she managed a smile.

He smiled back. And tossed and caught the ball. "Okay if I look in your yard for my other one?"

"Now?" said Iris. They headed down the road together. "Sure you can look in my backyard. I'll turn on the patio light so you can see better. Look in my backyard—look in my front yard! You can look anywhere you want."

The Trans Am screeched away.

"What's his problem?" said the boy.

Suddenly, Iris thought she might throw up. "See you!" she said to her neighbor, and hurried away.

Arriving home, Iris fumbled for her keys; where had she put them? It was practically dark. Why hadn't she remembered to turn on the lights before she left? She glanced over at the Blackmans' porch; the rocking chairs were empty. The lights were out.

Iris found the key in her pocket and unlocked the door.

She slammed it behind her and turned on the hall light. She flipped the switches for the porch light and the patio light.

Oh, God, thought Iris. *Why did I eat potato skins and ice cream?* She dropped her bag on the floor by the door and ran into the bathroom. She leaned over the toilet for a minute, with her hands on the seat.

She stared at the water and at the hole in the bottom of the bowl. Why did she eat onion rings? And ketchup! She looked at the water and gagged—but nothing came up.

Why did the man say he liked her? Why did he try to kiss her and say she loved it? She gagged again, but again nothing came up.

Why would a little kid love it if some creepy

man tried to kiss her? Iris stood up straight and took a few deep breaths of air.

What did she get in the car with a man for? She spat in the sink and looked in the mirror. Her breasts were enormous; she closed and locked the bathroom door and pulled off her sweatshirt and took off her bra and threw it under the bathroom sink. She shouldn't have bought a padded bra! The man thought she was sixteen years old, for heaven's sake!

He called her a slut!

If she hadn't gone to the mall for wolf-head underpants, this would never have happened. Why couldn't she just make a regular puppet out of a sock and felt and buttons, like Lydia or Hilary?

She put her sweatshirt back on and stood at the bathroom door with her hand on the doorknob, afraid to unlock it.

Tears came into Iris's eyes; she bit her lip. "Mommy!" she squeaked. "Mommy!" She covered her mouth with her hand, and tears ran down her face. "Please!" she cried. And she sat on the rim of the bathtub with her face in her hands, sobbing and shaking.

Then she stood up.

Someone was knocking on the front door!

ELEVEN

$\mathscr{I}$ris stopped breathing. The shoe salesman was banging on the door! What should she do? She wouldn't answer; she wouldn't answer, and he would go away.

Then she heard people talking on the steps outside. "Coming!" she called. She ran out of the bathroom and put her hand on the door handle. "Who is it?"

"Police," said a voice outside. "Open up!"

Was it really the police? Iris peered through the glass in the hall window. What were the police doing here? Had they come to arrest her?

Two men in beige police uniforms were standing in the porch light. They were wearing badges; there were guns in their holsters.

Iris unlocked the door and swung it open.

"Do you know this kid?" said one of the officers. "He says his name is Manuel—that he was looking for a baseball in your backyard—that he's your neighbor."

The boy next door was standing beside the police officer.

"Yes, he's my neighbor," said Iris.

"Well, the alarm went off down at the station," said the officer. "And we found him in the bushes by your basement window."

Iris groaned. "I forgot to turn it off; I came into the house. I forgot to turn the alarm off first."

The officer turned to his partner and shook his head. "Isn't this the second time this week we've been out here?"

"Or third," said his partner. "You can go now, pal," he said to Manuel. "Sorry about that—it's just that we don't see that many of you guys out here in this kind of a neighborhood."

Manuel brushed off his shirt; his sleeve was wrinkled where the policeman had been holding him.

"That many of *what* guys?" said a voice behind them.

The police officers turned. "I'm Dr. Rodriguez," said Manuel's father. "You don't see that many of *what* guys in neighborhoods like this?"

He put his arm around Manuel's shoulders. "Are you okay, son? What's going on here?"

One of the officers began to answer.

Dr. Rodriguez turned to the officer. "I'm talking to my boy. . . .

132

"Are you okay, Manuel?"

Manuel nodded.

"What's going on?" asked his father.

"I was looking in the bushes for my baseball—she said I could." He pointed to Iris. "I guess she set off the alarm."

"Sorry," said Iris. "I came home from the mall—I walked home. Then I let myself in with the key."

Manuel looked at Iris. "You walked home?"

Iris's heart skipped a beat. "Well . . . not the whole way. I rode home; a neighbor dropped me off . . . a friend of my mother's. Then I unlocked the door before I turned off the alarm."

"I guess we should take a look around," said one of the officers, "just to make sure. Take another look around the back of the house, would you?" he said to his partner. "I'll check the house. Anybody in the house?" he said to Iris.

"No," said Iris.

"Where are your parents?"

"They're not home . . . yet," said Iris.

"You're here alone?"

Iris's heart thumped. "Well, just for a couple of hours."

"How old are you?"

"Twelve and a half."

"Well, we would suggest that you be supervised by an adult, and you can tell your parents I said so."

Iris said nothing.

"Stay out here," he said to Iris, "while I check inside." And with his hand on his holster, he went into the house.

"Sorry," said Iris to Manuel and his father.

"No problem," said Dr. Rodriguez. He looked at Iris. "Are you all right?"

Iris nodded.

But she wasn't all right.

"You look a little shook up to me. You sure you're okay?"

Iris nodded. "Positive," she said, quietly.

"Well, if you'd like to come to our house to wait for your parents, you're more than welcome. My wife is repotting some plants—perhaps you'd like to help her. In any event, here's our number."

He handed Iris a little card with his name and the address of his office and the telephone numbers of his office and his residence on it.

"Thank you," said Iris, in a small voice.

The police officer walked back out onto the porch. "The house seems to be secure," he said. "But that's one helluva stuffed gorilla you've got in that bedroom; I practically drew my gun when I walked into the room."

He grinned at Dr. Rodriguez, but Dr. Rodriguez didn't smile.

"Headly," said Iris.

Everybody stared at her.

"His name is Headly."

Nobody said anything.

"My gorilla."

"Well, anyway," said the police officer, "try to remember the alarm, would you, young lady? We've been out here twice now."

"Sorry," said Iris.

"Okay back there," said the officer's partner, shining his flashlight at some bushes on the lawn and up into the tree branches above him.

"Well," said the officer on the porch. He tipped his hat to Dr. Rodriguez. "Good night, sir."

Dr. Rodriguez stared at him.

The police officer went to his car and, with the door open, began writing things on a sheet of paper attached to a clipboard.

Dr. Rodriguez stepped up to the car, his arm still around Manuel's shoulders. "Let me point out," he said, in a serious voice to the officer, "that you don't see many of any one person anywhere—unless you've got vision problems."

He reached in and tapped the clipboard. "There's only one of my son in the world," he said. "Make a note of it."

"And I'll call and make a note to his supervising officer," he said to Manuel as they turned and walked away.

Yes, there was only one Manuel Rodriguez.

And there was only one Iris Bloom.

And Iris had never felt more alone than when she closed the door behind her. Or more scared. Or more guilty.

Or more stupid for talking about Headly in front of the boy who lived next door.

She heard static on the police radio; a moment later, she heard the engine start. She looked out the window and watched the police car back out of the driveway and head down the road.

Iris lowered the blinds on the windows on either side of the door and twisted the clear plastic rods to close them. Good. Nobody could see in with the blinds closed. She hurried around the house, closing blinds and curtains in every room.

Then she went into her bedroom and sat down on the edge of her bed.

The house was quiet.

Iris stared at the floor. She got up from the bed and closed her door and pushed in the lock button on the handle. Never mind dinner; her stomach was still upset. She would just stay in her room, where she was safe. Just her and Ivy Lou. And tomorrow her parents would be home.

Iris felt a wave of fear. Boy. What if her parents found out she lied to Mrs. Fuller? What if they found out she'd gone alone to the mall?

How could they find out? They couldn't.

What would they think if they knew she'd taken a ride with the shoe salesman? How many times had they said not to take a ride with a stranger?

But the shoe salesman wasn't a stranger; he was a neighbor, a friend of her mother's. He'd sold them how many pairs of shoes?

Iris had no idea.

Besides, the salesman liked her; he thought she was sixteen years old. And who could blame him! She was acting so big, down at the mall by herself, walking home by herself. Of course he would think she was older—old enough to have a boyfriend. And he wanted to be her boyfriend; what was the harm in that? And what exactly did he do, anyway?

Iris could hardly remember. Had he tried to

kiss her? Or hadn't he; suddenly, Iris didn't know. Maybe she had imagined it. Or maybe it was an accident! Once, when she was in a hardware store, she had accidentally bumped rears with a boy when they had both leaned over on opposite sides of the aisle.

Had the shoe salesman tried to kiss her *on purpose?* Iris wasn't sure; she wasn't sure of anything, except that she was never going to wear a padded bra again.

She looked across the room into Ivy Lou's plexiglass box—at the pretty rock and at the purple shell. In a minute, she would go out and get Ivy Lou's new shell from the bag by the door. She yawned. Brother. Had it ever been a long day! She stared at Ivy Lou; finally, she was out of her shell.

But why was she so still? And pale!

Iris drew closer. Why was Ivy Lou hanging out of her shell and not moving? Iris picked her up; a leg fell off—just fell off into the gravel. Iris stared at Ivy Lou's face; her eyes were clouded.

She was dead.

How could it be? The day they left the pet shop, she was roaring around in the box like a lunatic—hanging half upside down from the crystal. She was scarfing up hermit chow and standing in her food dish—threatening Iris with her claw.

Iris felt angry. What a rip-off! Marge makes such a big deal about a hermit crab, and the next thing you know, it tips over. Iris picked up Ivy Lou and put her down again. Sick! Now she would have to bury her.

She opened the closet door. She needed a box—a box with a lid, for a coffin. She stared at the closet floor; what a mess! She got down on her knees and threw a football over her shoulder, threw a jacket over her shoulder. She hauled out the Monopoly game.

Under it she found a rubber boot, with half a dried-up peanut butter and jelly sandwich stuck to the sole; behind the boot she found a shoebox with her green sparkly flats wrapped in tissue paper inside. What ugly flats. Iris couldn't imagine why she bought them. She dumped them out of the box onto the floor, then chucked them into the back of the closet.

She set the box on her bed and rearranged the tissue paper inside it. There was a basket of silk flowers on top of her dresser; she tore a purple iris from its stem and put it into the box. Then she gently laid Ivy Lou's shell beside it. "See you, Ivy Lou," whispered Iris.

She put the lid on the box.

She would bury her in the yard tomorrow, when the sun came up.

Iris sat with the shoebox on her lap. *I'll sit here all night with a dead hermit crab in a box on my lap*, she thought sadly. *All alone.*

She sat on her bed, listening to the clock tick.

She heard cars drive down the street.

She heard a car door open and shut.

Quickly, Iris put the box on the rug and walked to the telephone. She dialed Maggie's father's number.

Maggie's little sister, Dinah, answered. "Is Maggie there?" asked Iris, in a shaky voice.

"Who is this?"

"Iris," said Iris.

Dinah said nothing.

"Can I talk to Maggie?" said Iris. "Please?"

Iris heard the phone clatter to the floor.

"Hello?" said Maggie, after a minute or two.

"It's Iris," said Iris. "Maggie?"

"What?"

"Can I come to your father's house?"

Maggie didn't answer.

"I know he doesn't like me, but—" Iris paused a minute, to gain control of her voice.

"Are you okay?"

"No," squeaked Iris.

"What's the matter!" cried Maggie.

"Just a minute!"

Maggie waited a minute.

"I just have to come over," whispered Iris. "I have to spend the night. I know it's his birthday—I know he wants to spend it with just you and Dinah! But something happened. And I'm . . . alone."

"You're home alone?" said Maggie. "Why isn't Mrs. Fuller there?"

Iris wiped her face on her sleeve. "Just don't ask," she whispered.

"Hold on," said Maggie.

Iris could hear Maggie talking to her father.

"Can she keep her hamster out of my briefcase this time?" Maggie's father was saying.

"Her hamster got away."

"Can she keep from feeding Dinah fish food?"

Iris's heart raced. She heard some whispering on the other end of the phone.

"He says yes," said Maggie.

"Pick me up as soon as you can," said Iris. "And Maggie?"

"What?"

"Ivy Lou croaked."

TWELVE

Iris peeked through the blinds. Where were Maggie and her father, anyway? A car drove slowly past her house.

Then all was quiet again, except for a dog barking.

Iris looked over at Manuel's house. A light was on in the potting shed; it illuminated part of the trellis near the door. Iris could see some flowers blooming in the dark.

She kept peering through the blinds.

Soon Maggie's father pulled into the driveway in his Mercedes and honked. Iris hurried out of the house and locked the door.

When she got to the car, she saw Dr. Rodriguez talking to Maggie's father. "—so," he was saying, "I thought I'd better come over and see who was in the driveway . . ."

Maggie's father reached out and shook his hand. "I'm sure the Blooms would appreciate it," he said.

"Hello, Iris," Dr. Rodriguez called, over the car top.

"Hello," said Iris. "I'm going to my best friend's house . . ."

"Yes, I know—have a good time," he said. "Nice meeting you," he said to Maggie's father. He waved and walked away.

Maggie turned around and watched as Iris climbed into the back seat of the car. "Hi," she said.

"Hi," said Iris. She put her backpack on the seat beside her and shut the door.

Dinah was sitting in the middle of the front seat, sucking her thumb and looking at nothing. Iris leaned forward and patted the top of her head.

"I thought you quit," said Iris.

"Tomorrow," said Dinah.

Iris put on her seat belt; they backed out of the driveway. "Happy birthday, Mr. Hunter," she said to Maggie's father.

"It's Sunday."

"How old will you be, anyway?"

"A hundred," said Maggie's father. He sighed out loud. "What's going on? Why were you home alone?"

"Well—" said Iris.

"Cut the crap," said Maggie's father.

"I lied to Mrs. Fuller," said Iris. "About when my parents are coming home; now she's gone to her sister's house in Vallejo—"

"And suddenly it dawned on you," interrupted Maggie's father, "that you're not ready to spend the night alone. Which is why your parents arranged for you to be with a baby-sitter." He looked in the rearview mirror and caught Iris's eye in the darkness. "Right?"

"Right," said Iris quietly.

"You're not equipped to be alone, Iris—you get into everything."

He slowed for a stop sign. "How old are you? Twelve?"

"No," said Iris. "I'm twelve and a half."

He turned right. "Well, let me ask you something." He paused. "What would you have done if we weren't home when you called?"

Iris didn't answer. What would she have done? She would have called the Blackmans as soon as they got home. Or called Maggie's mother; Maggie's mother would have helped her. Or she would have called Jennifer. Or Stella. Or maybe she would have gone over to Manuel Rodriguez's house. Would it have been okay to go over to Manuel Rodriguez's house and help his mother repot plants?

Were they strangers? Or were they neighbors? Iris didn't know.

"What would you have done, Iris?"

"I don't know," said Iris.

"Well, listen," said Maggie's father. "Don't get
me wrong: I'm happy to bail you out, kiddo—
and I'm glad you had the sense to call. But think
ahead next time, will you? Your parents expect
you to be under the care of an adult; you know
that."

Yes. Iris knew that.

"Don't you?"

"Yes!" said Iris.

"They're coming home tomorrow?"

"Yes."

"When?"

"About nine in the morning," said Iris.

"Well, let me tell you something, Iris. I'm going
to bring you home bright and early and wait
right there till they arrive, and when they do,
I'm going to tell them you ditched Mrs. Fuller."

Iris said nothing.

"Understand?"

"Yes," said Iris, in a quiet voice.

Maggie turned around and waved her hand in
the air behind the seat until Iris found it and
held on to it.

Maggie squeezed Iris's hand twice.

Iris squeezed Maggie's hand twice back.

Boy, it was good to have a friend! Iris's eyes got a little misty—lucky it was dark out. Tears ran down her cheeks and made her face itch—but she didn't move to wipe them. She just sat there holding on to Maggie's hand.

Soon they got to Maggie's father's house, and everybody got out of the car and went inside. "Have you eaten?" said Mr. Hunter to Iris.

"No," said Iris. "But I'm not really hungry. I had potato skins at the mall."

"You went to the mall?" said Maggie. "By yourself?"

Iris didn't answer.

Maggie's father shook his head. "Your parents and I are going to have *quite* a little chat in the morning."

"Where do I put this?" Iris asked, timidly. She held up her pack.

"My room," said Maggie. She followed Iris up the stairs. "Those are the socks?" she said. "I thought you said you couldn't get them."

They went into Maggie's room, Dinah following them. Iris looked down at her ankles and saw the skeleton socks sticking out of the tops of her sneakers. "These?" she said. She sat down and unlaced her shoes. "I forgot I had them on."

She took off her shoes and socks, and left the socks inside out on the rug.

"The guy at Sweet Feet gave them to me."

"He gave you socks?" said Maggie.

"Yup." Iris stood up and tossed the socks into the trash. "What do you want to do?"

"Why are you throwing them out?"

"I hate those socks, actually," said Iris.

"Why?" cried Maggie.

"Let's play Clue," said Iris. She took the Clue game from the top of the bookshelf and looked at the cover.

"Clue?" said Maggie. "Okay." She took the socks out of the trash. "I'll keep these if you don't want them."

"But they're gross!" said Iris. "Really! Look at them!"

Maggie turned the socks right side out and held them in the air in front of her. "They are?"

"Yes," said Iris. "Throw them away."

"I'll put them in my scrap bag," said Maggie. She pulled a plastic bag filled with scraps of material from under the bed. "Want to see the Canadian honker?"

She didn't wait for Iris to answer. She pulled out the Canadian honker and honked the head.

Iris heard a little muffled *Moop!* sound.

"It's good," said Iris.

Actually, it was more than good—it was perfect. It was a perfect goose with real feathers sewn on for the wings and tail.

"And like I said, all that's left to do is a beak," said Maggie.

"What about using two Lee press-on nails for the beak?" said Iris. "Use two thumbnails, and stick them on there somehow. I have some at my house." She paused. "I was saving them for when we have the band—but I don't think I'll be needing them. . . ."

"Lee press-on nails?" said Maggie.

"Yup. And I think my mom has some yellow nail polish in her dressing table drawer. She was a lemon on Halloween."

Maggie stared at the goose's face. "What do you think of fingernails for a beak?" she asked it.

She squeezed it twice and it *mooped* twice. Then she put it back into the scrap bag, along with the skeleton socks.

"How about your puppet? Did you get the underpants?"

"Yup."

"Well, how's it coming?"

"It's not," said Iris. "Let's play Clue."

"It's not?" said Maggie.

"Nope. I'm not going to make a wolf puppet," said Iris. "I'm not going to be in the puppet show. I don't want to trash Corky Newton's stupid puppet. I hate him and his puppet. I hate puppet shows and English class. I hate Mrs. Gersen."

Iris gazed into Maggie's eyes. "Let's play Clue, okay?"

Iris opened the Clue board on the rug and sat down. "I'm Miss Scarlet." She found the red marker. Maggie sat cross-legged opposite her.

Iris picked up the little metal weapons and set them on the board.

Maggie took the blue marker. "I'm Mrs. Peacock." She gathered the cards and sorted them into three piles. Iris watched while Maggie mixed up each of the piles and slid one card from each into the brown paper envelope.

"There," said Maggie.

Iris dealt out the rest of the cards. "Aren't we supposed to have three to play this game?"

Maggie shrugged. "Who cares? Roll the dice."

"We're supposed to have three to play this game. We need your father."

"No," said Maggie. "He hates Clue."

"What about Dinah?" said Iris.

Maggie stared at her. "Are you kidding? Just play. Roll the dice."

Iris shook the dice in her hand. She shook the dice and looked at Maggie. "If I tell you something, promise you won't tell anybody?"

"Roll the dice!" said Maggie.

Iris rolled a five and a two.

"Seven," said Maggie. "Yes, I promise."

She shook and rolled the dice. She rolled a four and a three.

"I mean *really* promise," said Iris.

"Okay! I really promise. Okay?"

"Swear to God?" said Iris.

"What *is* this?" said Maggie. She stared at Iris. "I *said* I promise."

Iris got up and closed the door. "You know the guy that gave me those socks?" She knelt down on the rug in front of Maggie. "Don't tell anybody this," said Iris. "Nobody. Cross your heart."

Maggie quickly crossed her heart. "Tell me!" she said.

"He said he likes me."

Maggie stared at her.

"He gave me a ride home from the mall today," said Iris. "It turns out he's a neighbor of ours." She picked up the little metal revolver and

looked at it in the palm of her hand. "He thought
I was sixteen."

Maggie watched Iris turn the gun in her hand.

"He stopped near the park; he wouldn't unlock the door of the car. Then he—" Iris paused.

"What!" whispered Maggie.

"It's really . . . gross," said Iris.

"Then he what?" said Maggie.

"He tried to kiss me. He said he liked me. But
don't tell anybody!"

Maggie brought her hand to her throat. "You're
kidding!"

"I'm not," said Iris. "And he said I loved it."

"Yuck!" cried Maggie.

Iris glanced over her shoulder at the door.
"Shhh!"

"That's sick!" whispered Maggie.

"I know," said Iris. "Shhh!"

Dinah was coming up the steps.

"You're supposed to 'Say no and tell!' when
somebody does something like that," whispered
Maggie.

"I did say no! And I banged on the window
and yelled and honked the horn till he let me
out of the car. Just shut up about it, okay?"

"But still!" said Maggie. "You're supposed to
tell your mom and dad!"

"Right," said Iris. " 'Oh, hi, Mom and Dad! Hope you had a nice trip. By the way, I lied to Mrs. Fuller and walked down to the mall, like I'm not supposed to do. To buy a padded bra.

" 'Then I got into a car with a guy, like I'm not supposed to do, and it turns out he's in love with me because he thinks I'm sixteen years old.' "

Maggie stared at Iris.

"Just don't worry about it, okay?" said Iris. "It doesn't have anything to do with you; it's my problem, okay?"

Maggie started to speak, but Iris frowned and put her finger on her lips. Dinah was turning the handle of the bedroom door. They waited for the door to open.

Dinah walked in. "Can I play?"

"No!" said Maggie. "Leave us alone—we're talking."

"Why can't I play?" said Dinah.

"You're too young to understand the game," said Maggie. "We've been through all this before; go watch TV. I think *Sesame Street*'s on."

"It is not."

"Well, something's on. Go see!"

Dinah sat on the rug and picked up the little metal wrench.

"Dad!" shouted Maggie. "Dinah won't leave us alone!"

Her father didn't answer.

Dinah picked up the dice and rolled them.

Maggie stood up. "I'm telling!" she said.

"Don't!" said Iris. "Wait! It doesn't matter—I don't want to play Clue, anyway." She shook the cards out of the envelope and picked them up. "See? I knew it! Miss Scarlet did it—in the conservatory. With the lead pipe. Let's go downstairs and watch TV with Dinah or something."

"And you're *not* picking the program!" Maggie said to Dinah.

They all went downstairs.

"Let's have a Tom Cruise festival," said Maggie. "Okay? I made Dad buy all of his movies—let's start with *Top Gun*. I haven't watched *Top Gun* in a long time, have you?"

Iris followed Maggie into the living room.

Maggie rooted through the video cabinet and found the *Top Gun* box and kissed it. She showed it to Iris. On the front was a picture of Tom Cruise wearing aviator sunglasses. "Isn't he totally gorgeous?" She held the box against her chest and swooned.

Maggie's father was sitting in an easy chair,

with a law brief in his lap, chewing on his pencil. "Don't tell me," he said. "Not again!"

Maggie ignored him. "He's jealous of Tom Cruise," she whispered, loudly. "Because his *fiancée,* Samantha, thinks Tom Cruise is cute!"

"What's this fiancée stuff?" said Maggie's father.

"Wait! I didn't show you!" cried Maggie. She jumped up and ran into the dining room and turned on the light. "See?"

Iris wandered in.

"My dress!"

The dress was spread out on the table like a cloud. "Don't move it," said Maggie. "It's pinned. Samantha's taking some tucks."

Iris stared at the dress.

Maggie fiddled with a spool of thread on the sewing machine while she talked. "Dinah's the flower girl. But she doesn't know yet. Just me and Dinah are in the wedding, and one of Samantha's law partners, and that's all."

Iris yawned. "Neat."

Maggie turned off the light.

"Well, anyway, that's the dress," said Maggie, quietly. She walked back into the living room, Iris following.

Maggie pushed the video into the VCR slot and pushed the PLAY button.

"I am *not*," said Maggie's father, "jealous of Tom Cruise; I'm sick of *Top Gun.*"

"Right, Dad," said Maggie. She rolled her eyes. "Look!" she cried as the movie started. "Here he is!" She turned to Iris. "Don't you just love him?"

Iris shrugged. No. She didn't love Tom Cruise; she didn't even know Tom Cruise. She sat on the couch in front of the TV and put her legs up.

Maggie's father looked over at her. "You sure you're not hungry?"

"Positive," said Iris. "In fact, my stomach feels a little . . . weird."

"Well, to tell you the truth," said Maggie's father, "you don't look so hot. You're sure you're doing okay?"

"I guess," said Iris.

But Iris wasn't sure she was doing okay. Why had she told Maggie what had happened? She wished she hadn't told her; now Maggie probably thought she was gross. She probably would end up hating her.

Iris began rubbing her arms; she had the shivers.

"You cold?" Maggie's father asked her. "Wait." He put his papers on the floor and stood up. Then he walked out of the room and came back with a big down comforter.

"Sit down, Mag," he said to Maggie. "Dinah! Sit by Maggie and Iris."

All the girls sat together on the couch. And Maggie's father covered them up.

Iris watched Tom Cruise fly upside down in his airplane, with his best friend, Goose, sitting behind him. Goose was the navigator.

Their friend, Cougar, was flying another airplane, beside them, and Cougar was freaking out.

Iris looked over at Maggie. "Take it easy," she said. "You've seen this part a million times; they all make it down okay."

Maggie didn't answer. She kept watching the movie, with her fists clenched in her lap.

Iris yawned and snuggled under the blanket.

The movie went on and on; planes dived in the air and chased each other. Tom Cruise and Goose were the champs. Tom Cruise had the guts, and Goose had the common sense; they were a team.

Dinah fell asleep; Maggie's father fell asleep and sat snoring in the chair, with his head tipped back against the wall.

Then it got to the sad part—the part where Goose dies. The airplane was in a flat spin; they couldn't pull it out.

It was going to go down.

They were yelling and trying to push the ejection button; one of them reached it.

Tom Cruise was thrown clear.

But Goose got slammed against the cockpit cover. Their parachutes opened, but when they landed in the water Goose was dead. Tom Cruise swam to him and held him in his arms. "No!" he shouted.

But Goose was dead.

"No!" he shouted again. Blood was dripping from Goose's head into the water.

A Coast Guard rescue helicopter was hovering overhead. A rescuer jumped into the water. "Sir," he yelled, "let go of him. You've got to let him go, sir!"

Then they pulled Goose's body up into the rescue helicopter on the end of a line.

Iris heard a little squeak on the couch beside her. She turned to see Maggie, sitting with her eyes closed, crying like a baby.

Iris pushed down the cover and reached over and touched Maggie's arm; but Maggie sat and sobbed. "It's okay, Maggie!" Iris whispered.

But Maggie shook her head no. No, it wasn't okay. Tom Cruise and Goose were best friends; they were a team.

And one of them was dead.

THIRTEEN

*I*ris?" whispered Maggie. "Iris!" She looked down over the rail of her bunk bed to where Iris was lying in a sleeping bag on the rug.

Iris didn't answer.

Quietly, Maggie climbed down the ladder. Dinah was asleep; her thumb was in her mouth. She began sucking loudly on it when Maggie reached the floor.

Iris was way down in the sleeping bag, with her head resting on the flannel bears. "Are you awake?" whispered Maggie.

Iris opened her eyes.

"I can't sleep," said Maggie. "I've been thinking: I don't think that guy from Sweet Feet thought you were sixteen."

Iris closed her eyes. "He did too!"

"He did not!" whispered Maggie. "Nobody thinks you're sixteen. You don't look sixteen. You look twelve. At the most!"

Iris turned her head away from Maggie. "Go to sleep."

"Even if you were sixteen," whispered Maggie,

"I don't think the guy was allowed to act like that. Why would he be allowed to act like that?"

Iris didn't answer; she didn't know the answer. She pretended to fall asleep. But Maggie just kept sitting beside her.

"I know you're awake," said Maggie.

Iris didn't move. Her eyelids fluttered; she concentrated on keeping them still and on keeping her breathing regular. She lay there a long time, waiting for Maggie to give up and go back to bed.

But Maggie didn't go back to bed.

"You're acting . . . weird," said Maggie. "It's scaring me!"

Iris kept breathing steadily. And after a few moments, Maggie began to cry. She sat there in the dark, sniffing and swallowing. She wiped her eyes on the sleeve of her nightgown.

Iris sat up on her elbow. "*Now* what's the matter?"

"Oh, I don't know," said Maggie.

It was dark; Iris could barely make out Maggie's face.

"You don't like my bridesmaid's dress."

"Yes, I do!"

"No, you don't. You don't have to say you do when you don't."

"God," said Iris.

"Don't you hate it when Goose dies?" said Maggie. "In *Top Gun?*"

"Yes," said Iris. "But why do you keep crying about it!"

"I don't know!" whispered Maggie. She wiped her nose on the hem of her nightgown. "I cry every time. They were such good friends! They were like you and me! It makes me so sad!" she squeaked. "Why does something bad have to happen to Goose?"

"Stop crying," said Iris. "It's only a movie, Mag—it's only some story somebody dreamed up." She reached out and tugged on Maggie's sleeve. "Stop crying, okay? In real life, nobody dies—"

"Yes, they do!"

"But not Goose! Goose doesn't die—he walks off the set and goes to the bank and deposits a check for a million dollars and drives over to Tom Cruise's house in a Ferrari. And they put their feet up on the coffee table and drink Pepsis and eat corn chips. And squeeze the cheese."

Maggie pulled her nightgown over her knees and leaned her chin on it. "Oh, they do not."

"Yes, they do. They sit there eating chips and launching air biscuits—"

"Oh, shut up." Maggie tipped her head sideways and stared at Iris in the dark. "You know," she whispered after a while, "I don't know what I would ever do without you for a friend."

Iris said nothing.

Maggie closed her eyes. "I really mean it!"

"Well, nothing's going to happen to me—"

"Something did happen to you!"

"No, it didn't," said Iris. "Shut up about it, okay? I'm fine!"

"You're not fine!" said Maggie. "You won't trash Corky Newton's puppet! You call that fine? Everybody's depending on you—Jennifer even called and told me."

Iris yawned.

"You're wimping out on everybody. . . . And you won't tell your mom and dad about the guy from Sweet Feet. What if he . . . comes after you?"

Iris's heart thumped.

"What if the guy's a psycho!"

"Stop trying to freak me out!" said Iris. "Jeez! I shouldn't have even told you. You're making such a big deal out of everything."

"I know, but—"

"You don't know! It's over! Nothing happened! So forget it, okay? You're going to wake up Dinah. He's not coming after me. He said just keep my mouth shut—which I should have done. Just you keep your mouth shut, and we'll all be fine."

Maggie sat in the dark. She peeled part of her little toenail off. "Well, I don't feel fine."

"Let me go back to sleep, Maggie. Please!" said Iris. "I'm just so tired!"

Maggie stood up and looked out her bedroom window; she could see the position lights of an airplane flying through the darkness.

Below her, the living room light was still on; it lit the bushes on the pathway to the front door of her father's house. "I'm hungry," she whispered. "Are you hungry?"

"No. I want to go to sleep."

"There are Mrs. Fields cookies downstairs," said Maggie. "You don't want a chocolate-chip cookie with macadamia nuts?"

"No!" Iris sat up for a minute and zipped the zipper of the sleeping bag a little farther up, then lay back down again.

"See?" said Maggie. "You won't even eat a chocolate-chip cookie."

Iris said nothing. She snuggled way, way down into the bag. Soon she was asleep.

She dreamed of rattlesnakes. She ran! But they slithered after her. She jumped over a fallen log.

There was a hole in it; she crawled inside. She couldn't fit all the way in, though. She couldn't get her hand in. She saw rattlesnakes lash by—one stopped and looked into her eyes and flicked out his tongue. He was coiled and ready to strike!

Then the log was in a lake; she was floating facedown in the lake. Her face was in the water. She couldn't lift it up. Below her, on the murky river bottom, she saw skeletons lifting their bony fingers and pointing in her direction. A lavender life preserver floated by; she couldn't grab it. She was going under! She couldn't breathe!

Iris burst from her sleeping bag, sweating and gasping for air. Her heart was racing; she felt sick and tired. There was an ache in her chest and her stomach. It had been there since the day before. She wished it would go away.

She stared across the rug at Dinah, asleep in the bottom bunk; the top bunk was empty. Iris looked up at the window. The sky was pink.

Where was Maggie?

Iris got up and went into the bathroom to pee. Maggie's father's bathrobe was hanging from a hook on the back of the door. She didn't suppose he'd mind if she put it on. Climbing into it, she tied the terry cloth belt around her waist and closed up the front almost all the way to her chin. There. She felt like a sumo wrestler.

A little one.

Iris turned on the faucet and washed her hands. Could you get AIDS if someone put his mouth on your hand?

She washed her hands again.

She heard a woman's voice downstairs. Maybe Samantha had come over. She dried her hands on the robe and walked to the top of the stairs. "Maggie?"

Iris walked down the stairs. Could anybody see up her nightgown as she walked down the stairs? No one was looking; still, she guarded her legs by holding the robe closed.

Maggie and her father were sitting at the kitchen table, drinking tea. Iris looked at the clock.

"Morning, Iris," said Maggie's father. He stood up as she walked into the room. "We're all early birds this morning."

Iris looked at Maggie, who looked away.

Then Maggie's mother appeared in the doorway.

What was *she* doing at Maggie's father's house—at seven o'clock in the morning?

"Hello, Iris," she said quietly.

"It's just a very, very pretty dress," she said to Maggie. "It's beautiful! Did you see it, Iris?"

Iris nodded.

"It will look pretty on Maggie, don't you think? Good with her hair?"

Iris nodded. *What* was going on?

Maggie's mother walked over to where Maggie was sitting and stood behind her, gathering back her hair. "What shoes will you wear?"

"I'm not sure," said Maggie. "Samantha was wondering about little heels."

"That's a possibility," said Maggie's mother. "But what about flats, dyed to match?" She looked up at Maggie's father and smiled a little. "It's a long way down the aisle in high-heeled shoes—for an eleven-year-old."

She kissed the top of Maggie's head.

And turned to Iris. "Iris," she said, gently. "Sit down."

Maggie's father pulled another chair up to the table. "I'll be in the living room if anybody needs me," he said. He put his hand on Maggie's mother's shoulder, and then he left the room.

Iris looked again at Maggie. But Maggie couldn't look at Iris; she just stared down at her tea. Iris sat on the edge of the chair and folded her hands in front of her on the table. Maggie's mother reached over and covered up Iris's hands with her hands.

Suddenly, Iris knew what was coming.

"Maggie and her father called me this morning," she began. "Maggie told me what happened."

Iris glanced over at Maggie. She couldn't believe it; Maggie had told her mother and father everything.

"Sorry," said Maggie. "I'm sorry!"

"Right," said Iris.

"I am!" said Maggie.

"She is sorry," said Maggie's mother. "It's hard to break a promise to a friend." She looked over at Maggie in a sympathetic way and then back again at Iris. "You understand that . . ."

Iris looked away.

"Don't you?"

No. Iris didn't understand anything. She was just a total jerk; and her best friend had told her worst secret to her mother and father. She pulled her hands away.

"You lied to Mrs. Fuller—"

Iris stood up, and Maggie's mother stood up with her.

"Let me finish!" she said.

Iris stared at Maggie.

"I *said* I'm sorry," said Maggie.

"Let me finish!" said Maggie's mother again. "And you went to the mall alone, which you're not allowed to do. And you started to walk home alone. . . ."

Iris stared at the ceiling.

"Iris, are you listening to me? You made some bad decisions. You didn't use good judgment. . . ."

Iris just stood there, feeling numb. Maggie had told her mother? Iris couldn't believe Maggie had actually told her mother!

"Still, what the man did wasn't your fault. . . . You made some good decisions too," said Maggie's mother. "Sit down, Iris."

Iris sat down and tried to look bored.

"You made some good decisions, like yelling! And banging on the window and honking the horn to make him let you out. That was good thinking. It may have saved you from . . . other things happening."

"Do we have to talk about this?"

"Yes," said Maggie's mother. "And I'm going to say it again: It wasn't your fault, Iris. The guy has a problem about wanting to take advantage of kids."

"Well, I'm not exactly a kid," said Iris.

"Yes, you are. You are exactly a kid."

"He thought I was sixteen," said Iris. "He's a neighbor!"

"No, he didn't, Iris. Nobody thinks you're sixteen. Everybody thinks you're twelve years old. You're a twelve-year-old girl, barely out of elementary school and full of beans. The man knew that.

"And he isn't a neighbor, either. Maggie's father has connections. He had an investigator from the district attorney's office up at dawn, running a background check on him. No way is that guy a neighbor—he lives in a condominium over by the high school. And he's had problems with this kind of behavior before, in another city."

"He had somebody check into it?" said Iris.

"Well, you don't think Maggie's father would let somebody pull something like that on you, do you, Iris? And get away with it?"

Iris thought a minute.

No, Maggie's father wouldn't let anybody get away with anything.

"And," said Maggie's mother, "since this man has had a problem with kids in the past, he's not allowed to give rides to people under eighteen. So now he's in trouble with the police—

again—but that's his problem. And he has to face it. . . . He's just a loser, Iris."

Iris rested her head on her arm and closed her eyes.

"It's easy to confuse somebody who's twelve, to scare somebody who's twelve. But he has to deal with adults now—adults who aren't afraid of him. Who would never let him hurt you—never let him near you. . . . Now he's the one who's scared."

Maggie's mother softly patted Iris's back. "Have a little sympathy for yourself, Iris."

Tears sprang into Iris's eyes.

"It's not the kid's fault when this happens. Didn't you learn that in school?"

No. She didn't learn that in school. Was that kind of thing supposed to be taught in school? She had learned about not taking a ride with a stranger from TV; but the shoe salesman wasn't a stranger.

"Do you think I'll get AIDS?" she said.

"AIDS?" said Maggie's mother.

She paused.

"Is there anything else that happened that you didn't tell Maggie—that we don't know about?"

"No," whispered Iris.

"Then you can't get AIDS," said Maggie's mother.

Well, that was good. It made Iris feel a little better, knowing that she wasn't going to die of AIDS.

She began to cry, and Maggie and her mother just sat there with her, patting her back and saying nothing.

"I have to blow my nose," she said, after a while.

Maggie quickly grabbed a napkin from the basket on the table and handed it to Iris.

Iris frowned at her and blew her nose.

"Soon your mother and father will be home. And when they come home, we will be waiting for them: you, Maggie, and me. Okay?"

"No!" said Iris.

Maggie's mother put her hand on her arm. "Iris, they need to know."

Iris suddenly stood up. "They don't need to know! Why do they need to know? Why?"

Maggie's mother didn't answer. She put her arms around Iris. And at first, Iris just stood there.

"Because you need them to know," said Maggie's mother.

A bird sang outside the window.

"Somebody did something like that to me once too," said Maggie's mother.

Then Iris let Maggie's mother hold her. She rested her head on her sweater—it felt good to be in somebody's arms.

"I'm sorry, Iris," said Maggie's mother. And Iris felt her tremble a little. She stared past her shoulder into Maggie's eyes.

"Don't cry, Mom," said Maggie.

FOURTEEN

I don't want to have the band," said Iris, quietly. "It's just a stupid idea—we could never have a band that was any good."

Maggie said nothing.

"You can have the stockings," said Iris. "You can have both pairs of the stockings my mom is bringing back and both the garter belts; I hate garter belts and stockings. And I don't feel like being in a band. And the miniskirts!"

Maggie sighed. "Okay . . . if that's how you feel about it."

"That's how I feel about it," said Iris.

They stared at each other for a moment, then Iris turned away.

"I *was* going to surprise you with something, though: Dad is renting a saxophone for me—" said Maggie.

"I told you," said Iris. "I don't want to have the band."

"I had one lesson the weekend before last at Zone Music," continued Maggie. "They give one lesson free. The guy said I was a natural."

172

Iris shoved her nightgown into her pack. "Um-hmm."

"Dad was waiting in the keyboard room. He said he thought I sounded like a goose got run over." Maggie looked at Iris to see if she would laugh.

But Iris didn't laugh. "I'm just not into having a band anymore, okay? Play the saxophone with somebody else," she said.

"And also," continued Maggie, "Dad ordered me a tape with a band on it—you play along with it. It's for beginning alto sax players. It even has a Paula Abdul song on it."

"Good," said Iris. "Then you don't need a band. You can play along with Paula Abdul."

"I do too need a band!"

"Well, have a band with somebody else. Call up Corky Newton—ask him to bring his tuba." Iris folded the sleeping bag in half and started to roll it up.

"Never mind the sleeping bag," Maggie told her. "Let's go. Wait! I forgot my Canadian honker. Is it still okay to make the beak at your house? Is it still okay to have the press-on nails?"

"I guess," said Iris. She walked out of the bedroom and down the stairs, with Maggie following her.

Maggie's mother and father were standing by

the front door. "I'll talk to you later," said Maggie's mother.

"Thanks," said her father.

He looked over at Iris. "I'm glad you thought to call and come here last night."

"Right," said Iris. "Happy birthday," she told him, as she walked out.

"It's tomorrow," said Maggie's father. "And I want a Lamborghini!" he called from the doorway. "A black one."

Iris, Maggie, and Maggie's mother got into the car. "Do I need to bring glue?" Maggie quietly asked Iris.

"No," said Iris.

"All set?" said Maggie's mother.

Maggie made small talk with her mother, while Iris sat frowning and looking out the window.

". . . and Iris has press-on nails she's giving me for the Canadian honker," said Maggie. "For the beak! And yellow nail polish—her mother was a lemon on Halloween."

Maggie's mother glanced over at Iris. She looked so sleepy. She looked the way she did when she was little, when the girls were at preschool together.

Her hair was even matted in the back, like Dinah's.

"Hey, Iris!" whispered Maggie's mother. "Wake up!"

Iris faked a smile.

Maggie cheerily pointed out things along the way: a Volkswagen with a plaster banana on top, a man with a handlebar mustache, a black Labrador retriever with part of a blackberry vine stuck in its tail.

Iris ignored her. And when they got to her house, she was the first one out of the car. "I'll unlock the door," she told Maggie's mother, politely.

Maggie and her mother visited with each other on the porch while Iris turned off the burglar alarm and opened the door.

She went upstairs.

Soon Maggie came in. "Where are you?" She looked in the living room.

"I'm up here," said Iris. She slowly walked halfway down the stairs. "I couldn't find the yellow nail polish. But here's these. . . ." She tossed Maggie the box of Lee press-on nails.

Iris sat on the stairs and gazed at the floor.

Maggie came and sat beside her. "I said I was sorry I told." She began picking at her thumbnail. "But I'm not. You know? I'm really not." She looked at Iris, but Iris just kept looking down at the floor. "I'm sorry it happened. But I'm not sorry I told, and I've been wondering—wouldn't you have told if it had been me?"

Iris didn't answer. They both stared through the doorway into the kitchen, looking at nothing.

"I know you're not going to make the wolf puppet," said Maggie, "but could I see the underpants, anyway? I want to see what they look like up close."

Iris pointed to a crumpled-up paper bag near the front door, and Maggie walked down and picked it up. She came back to where Iris sat and opened the bag; she peered inside. "Holy cow!" she said. "Are these great!" She shook everything in the bag out onto the stairs and held the satin underpants in the air. The empty hermit crab shell rolled from step to step until it reached the floor.

Iris just sat there looking at it, with her arms wrapped around her knees.

"Too bad Ivy Lou croaked," said Maggie. "You could have let her crawl up into Corky Newton's puppet's head and latch onto his finger during the puppet show."

"You don't think I thought of that?" said Iris.

Maggie put the underpants on the step beside

her, then she rooted around in her pocket and pulled out one skeleton sock. She plunged her hand into it and stretched it up past her elbow. "If we were going to make the wolf puppet, we would blacken out the skeletons with a felt tip pen," she said, in a soft voice. "Do you have a felt tip pen?"

Iris shrugged. "There might be one in the hat stand."

Maggie went down to the hat stand and opened the drawer. She rummaged through it.

"Or in the basket on the kitchen counter," said Iris.

Maggie went into the kitchen, and Iris heard her shuffling through the papers in the basket. "Aha!" she heard Maggie say. Then Maggie came back in, holding a wide-tipped permanent marker, and sat beside Iris. She slowly began blotting out the skeletons.

Iris picked up one of the little packages of ketchup that Maggie had dumped out of the bag. "You really think it would have been a good idea to get ketchup on Corky Newton's puppet?"

"Yup," said Maggie.

"Even though it cost two hundred dollars?"

"Can it be dry cleaned?" said Maggie.

"I don't know," said Iris.

"Find out," said Maggie, in a sly way. "Find out! If it can't be dry cleaned, if the stains *can't* be removed . . ."

Iris stared at her.

"Then do it for sure," said Maggie. "And there's something else I'd like to find out." She looked at Iris for a long time. "How much damage do you think your mom and dad could do to a red Trans Am . . . with a sledgehammer?"

"I don't know," said Iris. "I'll have to ask them." She tossed the ketchup package and caught it. "Guess what?"

"What?"

"I started my period—I was lying to you before. I don't know why."

"Oh," said Maggie. "Well, congratulations."

"You're the only one who knows," said Iris. "And *don't* tell anybody."

"Why would I tell anybody?" said Maggie. "Anyway," she said, shaking the wolf-head underpants at Iris, "what would you stuff the wolf's nose with if you were going to make this puppet? Cotton? Or what?"

Iris didn't answer.

"Think," said Maggie. "What would Arthur Frisco suggest?" She tapped the side of her head and made a nerdy expression.

Iris stood up and stretched and walked down into the bathroom. "Those underpants growl too, you know."

Maggie heard her peeing, and she heard the toilet flush and the water in the sink run and the bathroom cabinet open and shut.

Iris came out with her hand behind her back. "Arthur Frisco would suggest"—she made trumpet noises and held up the padded bra— "this!" She squeezed the cups. "These are filled with foam rubber."

"Cut that up?" said Maggie. "Are you kidding?" She snatched the bra from Iris. "No way!" she cried. "I've been needing a bra like this for years. *Years!*"

Maggie stood up and threw off her shirt. She put the bra around her waist like a belt and did the clasp, then whirled it around and adjusted the straps. She put her shirt back on. "How do I look?"

"You look like an eleven-year-old wearing a padded bra," said Iris.

"So," said Maggie, "I *am* an eleven-year-old wearing a padded bra. Is there a law against that?"

"No, but you look ridiculous."

"I do not. Now! You really *do* need to find

something to stuff the wolf-head with," said Maggie. "I'm not kidding you, Iris. I've *got* to see this wolf-head stuffed."

Iris sighed. "There might be some cotton balls under my bed, with the nail polish stuff," she said, after a while. "I don't know. . . . But I doubt it!" she called.

Maggie had hurried into the bedroom. "Where'd you get all the nail polishes?"

Iris didn't answer.

"Neons!" Maggie cried.

"Yup," said Iris. "And neon lipstick. Which is under there somewhere." She stood up. Through the window, she could see Manuel Rodriguez tossing his baseball and catching it in his mitt.

Iris looked at the reflection of her face in the glass on the clock that was ticking in the hall. She looked good.

She fixed her bangs a little. "But I'm warning you," she called to Maggie. "Neon lipstick will screw up the mouthpiece on a saxophone."

"Well, you would be the one to know about lipstick and mouthpieces," called Maggie, "after what you did to Corky's tuba last year."

"Well, I'm just telling you," said Iris. "Do *not* plan on wearing neon lipstick in the band." She paused. "I will be the only one wearing neon lipstick in the band."

The house grew very quiet. Iris looked out the window again at Manuel. What a hunk!

"I'm thirsty!" called Maggie. "Bring in something to drink. And those corn chips I saw in the kitchen!"

"Yes, *ma'am!*" said Iris. She wandered into the kitchen. *"And!"* she called to Maggie. "Don't get too attached to that bra." She pulled two cans of Pepsi out of the refrigerator and took them into the bedroom. She dropped the chips onto the bed and put the Pepsis on her desk and popped them open. "Did you hear what I said? I'm not necessarily giving you that bra. You need to uphold the standards of the presidency of The Flat People's Club. . . ."

"Shhh!" said Maggie. She was standing at the window.

"I hope you know my neighbor may have seen you put that bra on," said Iris.

"Will you *listen?* Listen! What's that noise?"

They looked at each other. They heard a faint scratching sound. "You can't hear that?" said Maggie.

Iris frowned. "It's the Fritos bag unwrinkling."

"It is not," said Maggie. "Shhh!"

Iris walked closer to the window. "It's out there," she said.

"No, it isn't," said Maggie. For a moment, neither spoke. "It's inside," whispered Maggie. They heard scratching again, and rustling. "And it better not be a mouse."

Suddenly, Iris leaned down. She picked up the shoebox. She took off the lid and looked inside. Ivy Lou was standing on the tissue paper, trying to climb up the cardboard corner of the box. Near her were empty claws and feet, an empty body—with tiny cloudy empty eyes on posts.

Iris turned to Maggie. "She's still alive?" She picked up Ivy Lou's shell, and Ivy Lou darted back inside. Iris saw tips of feet and a fat new pink claw. "What's going on? How could she be alive again?"

"You dork!" said Maggie. "She molted! Crabs molt. Didn't you know that crabs molt?"

No. Iris didn't know that crabs molted; she knew a lot of things, but she didn't know that crabs molted.

"Apparently, you didn't listen last year when Arthur Frisco gave his science report on crustaceans," said Maggie.

"Apparently not," said Iris. "I can't believe this! I thought she was dead!" She clutched Ivy Lou's shell against her heart. Then she opened up her hand a little and peered down at it. "Good thing you made some noise, you dope!" she said to Ivy Lou. "Good thing Maggie heard you!" She looked at Maggie. "I was going to bury her, you know—"

"But you didn't," said Maggie. She moved closer to Iris. "So she's fine. And you're fine— and I'm fine. And everything's fine. Give her to me." She took Ivy Lou and looked into the shell. "Get your butt out of there," she whispered. Two pink pointy legs moved a little. Her claw opened.

"Look out . . ." said Iris.

Mavis Jukes was a teacher and a lawyer before she started writing books for children. She is the author of *Like Jake and Me*, a Newbery Honor Book, *Blackberries in the Dark*, *No One Is Going to Nashville*, *Lights Around the Palm*, and *Getting Even*—her first novel. She lives with her artist husband and two daughters in Sonoma County, California.